JOIN THE FUN
IN CABIN SIX . . .

KATIE   is the perfect team player. She loves competitive games, planned activities, and coming up with her own great ideas.

MEGAN   would rather lose herself in fantasyland than get into organized fun.

SARAH   would be much happier if she could spend her time reading instead of exerting herself.

ERIN   is much more interested in boys, clothes, and makeup than in playing kids' games at camp.

TRINA   hates conflicts. She just wants everyone to be happy . . .

AND THEY ARE! Despite all their differences, the Cabin Six bunch are having the time of their lives at CAMP SUNNYSIDE!

MARILYN KAYE is the author of many popular books for young readers, including the "Out of This World" series and the "Sisters" books. She is an associate professor at St. John's University and lives in Brooklyn, New York.

Camp Sunnyside is the camp Marilyn Kaye wishes that she had gone to every summer when she was a kid.

CAMP SUNNYSIDE FRIENDS #9

The New-and-Improved Sarah

Marilyn Kaye

AN AVON CAMELOT BOOK

CAMP SUNNYSIDE FRIENDS #9: THE NEW-AND-IMPROVED SARAH is an original publication of Avon Books. This work has never before appeared in book form.

AVON BOOKS
A division of
The Hearst Corporation
105 Madison Avenue
New York, New York 10016

First Avon Camelot Printing: September 1990

CAMELOT TRADEMARK REG. U.S. PAT. OFF. AND IN OTHER COUNTRIES, MARCA REGISTRADA, HECHO EN U.S.A.

Printed in the U.S.A.

OPM 10 9 8 7 6 5 4 3 2 1

For Tova Gold

The New-and-Improved Sarah

Chapter 1

It was the bottom of the ninth inning, and the bases were loaded, with two outs. On the Camp Eagle softball field, a Camp Sunnyside girl stood on each base, poised to run.

"This is so exciting!" Megan squealed. "If we get all those girls home, we're going to win! We're actually going to beat the boys!"

Katie didn't act quite as excited. "Yeah, I know. But look who's up at bat."

Katie spoke in a whisper, but Sarah heard her remark. She approached the base, dragging the bat behind her. "Okay, don't rub it in. I know I'm not the greatest hitter." She gazed out at the field glumly. Here they were, at their first big competition with the boys' camp. Whether the Sunnyside girls won or lost was entirely on her shoulders. And she knew what

1

Katie knew, what all the cabin six girls on the team knew. There was no way she could pull this off.

Her cabin mates smiled encouragingly, and the rest of the Sunnyside team was cheering. "C'mon, Sarah! Bring 'em home!" It only made her feel worse.

"Couldn't we get someone else to bat now?" she asked Katie. "One of the cabin seven girls, maybe?"

Katie shook her head sadly. "It's against the rules. No pinch hitters." A look of defeat was already clear on her face.

Sarah knew how much Katie hated to lose. "I'm sorry, Katie."

"It's not your fault." Katie sighed in resignation. "Just do your best."

Out in the backfield, the Camp Eagle boys were getting tired of waiting. "Go! Go! Go!" they chanted.

Sarah turned and gave the Sunnyside team an apologetic look. Trina smiled in sympathy. Erin just shrugged, with a who cares expression. She'd struck out earlier in the game. But at least no one had been on base.

Sarah got into position. The Camp Eagle pitcher threw the ball. Sarah swung the bat. It didn't even come close to making contact with the ball.

The counselor who was acting as the umpire yelled, "Strike one!"

Sarah gritted her teeth. That didn't help. Her next effort produced exactly the same result.

"Strike two!"

For the third time, Sarah raised the bat. She tried very hard to block out the yelling and the eyes watching her. She concentrated on the ball and told herself, I'm going to hit this one. But her inner voice wasn't very confident. And for good reason. The ball flew past her before she could even go into her swing.

The umpire's cry of "Strike three" was drowned out by the cheers from the Camp Eagle boys.

There were no cheers behind Sarah. Sarah steeled herself to turn and face the team. At least her cabin mates didn't look angry. But the other girls on the team weren't as forgiving.

"You didn't even try to hit it," one girl accused her.

"Yeah, and it was an easy pitch," another shouted.

Megan rushed to Sarah's defense. "Don't yell at her! Sarah's just not all that good at softball."

3

"She did her best," Trina added.

Even Katie was being a good sport. "It was just bad luck that it was her turn at bat."

Her friends' words were comforting. They understood her. And when a girl from cabin seven snapped, "You better practice before the next game," Sarah wasn't terribly hurt. She knew all the practice in the world wouldn't help. Like Megan had said, she just wasn't any good at softball. Or any other sport, for that matter.

The team began to drift away, leaving the cabin six girls together. Megan put an arm around Sarah's shoulder. "Don't feel bad." Sarah smiled at her best friend.

"We probably wouldn't have won anyway," Erin remarked.

"Why not?" Trina asked.

"Because boys are just better at sports than girls."

"That's not true!" Katie exclaimed.

Megan nodded vigorously. "I've beaten boys lots of times at tennis."

"Okay," Erin relented. "Maybe girls can be just as good. But it's still better for us if we lose."

Katie looked at Erin as if the fair-haired girl had lost her mind. "Good grief! Why?"

4

The smug, know-it-all smile that was Erin's trademark appeared on her face. "Boys hate to lose to girls. They like to feel superior. If you want to get along with a boy, you have to let him win."

"That's ridiculous," Katie stormed. Her eyes narrowed. "Did you strike out before on purpose?"

"Maybe," Erin said. "Look, Katie, I've had more experience with boys than you have."

"Hah!" Katie retorted. "I've got two brothers!"

Erin patted Katie's shoulder. "I'm talking about romantic experience."

Megan rolled her eyes. "Can we go eat? I'm starving." They headed across the field to the area where the two camps were gathered for a picnic.

"Why do we have to have all these activities at Camp Eagle anyway?" Sarah asked mournfully. "We've got our own camp."

Megan spoke in a squeaky, high-pitched voice. "Because it's important for boys and girls to have recreational interaction. It promotes healthy relationships."

Everyone laughed at Megan's impersonation of Ms. Winkle, the Camp Sunnyside director.

"Personally, I like playing against boys," Katie said, shooting a look at Erin. "Oh course, I like it better when we win. No offense, Sarah."

"That's okay," Sarah said. "But we'll never win as long as I'm on the softball team. Or the volleyball team or the swimming team or any other team for that matter."

"Don't worry," Trina said in a soothing manner. "There are other things you're good at."

"Oh yeah?" Sarah said. "Like what?"

"Reading," Trina replied. "You're the fastest reader in the cabin. How many books have you read so far this summer?"

Sarah had lost count. "A lot. But I don't think we're going to have a reading competition with Eagle."

"I don't understand you guys," Erin said. "Here we are, surrounded by boys, and all you can think about is competing with them."

"You were pretty happy when Ms. Winkle announced we'd be having more activities with Eagle," Megan pointed out.

"For a very different reason," Erin said. She surveyed the groups gathered around the picnic area. "Watch and see." She sauntered across the grass, passing a group of boys. She gave them a casual glance. A moment later, two of the boys left their group and started walking toward her.

6

The other girls watched. "I've never known anyone as boy crazy as Erin," Katie remarked.

"Just look at her," Sarah marveled. "How can she look so good after playing softball?"

"Because she didn't *do* anything," Megan retorted. "Did you see her when we were in the outfield? She barely moved! She never ran after any balls."

It certainly paid off for her, Sarah thought. While the rest of them were sweaty and dirty, Erin was immaculate. Her tee shirt wasn't even wrinkled. Sarah gazed in wonder as Erin talked to the two boys, tossing her head and laughing.

The others were watching too. "What a flirt," Katie commented. "It's disgusting."

"I don't think it's so disgusting," Sarah murmured.

"C'mon, let's get some food," Megan urged.

Camp Eagle had laid out a huge spread. Sarah counted at least five kinds of sandwiches, plus potato salad, macaroni salad, and three-bean salad. And the desserts were incredible. There were brownies and cookies of every possible type. She had a hard time choosing. Finally, she gave up and took a little of everything.

She had to carry her plate with both hands as she left the food table. When Erin saw the contents of Sarah's plate, she shook her head and frowned. "You're going to get fat."

Erin's plate bore no resemblance to Sarah's. She had half a sandwich and a tiny scoop of salad. No wonder she's got such a great figure, Sarah thought enviously.

"Let's grab that bench over there," Katie said.

"Bobby wants me to eat with him," Erin said. "See you guys later."

Sarah went with the others to the picnic bench. But she kept looking over her shoulder at Erin. "Why are boys so crazy about her?"

"Well, she's beautiful," Megan pointed out.

"We know that," Katie said. "She's always reminding us."

Trina eyed Erin thoughtfully. "I read in a magazine once that any girl can be beautiful if she knows how to fix herself up right."

"But she's got something else, besides being beautiful," Sarah said. "She knows how to act around boys. They all end up thinking she's special."

"I think that's because she tells them what they want to hear," Trina said. "So she makes *them* feel special."

Katie groaned. "Boys already think they're special. They don't need any encouragement."

She turned to a boy who was coming from the food table. "Hey, Justin!"

Justin came by their bench and paused. "Hi!"

"Congratulations on winning the game," Katie said. Before Justin could thank her, she quickly added, "But you should work on your pitching. Your curve ball wasn't very curvy."

Justin nodded. "Yeah, I know. Maybe you can practice with me sometime."

Katie nodded graciously. "Glad to."

"Great." Justin moved on to join some boys at another bench. Katie turned to her cabin mates.

"See? It's good for them to hear some criticism."

Sarah had to admit that Justin seemed to admire Katie. But he didn't look at her the way boys looked at Erin. She turned once more and gazed at Erin. There was a boy sitting with her and Bobby who looked really cute.

"Why do you keep looking over there?" Megan asked.

"No reason," Sarah said.

Megan looked suspicious. "You're not jealous of her, are you? Think about what Erin has to go through to be the way she is. Always fussing with her hair, putting on makeup, doing her

9

silly act . . . it all sounds like a lot of hard work to me. I wouldn't want to be like her."

"And you shouldn't," Trina said. "You should be happy being just who you are."

"That's right," Katie said.

But Sarah wasn't so sure.

Later that afternoon, when the campers returned to Sunnyside, the girls went directly to cabin six to wash up before dinner. Their counselor greeted them warmly.

"Did you guys have a good time at Eagle?" Carolyn asked.

"Great," Katie told her. "Except we lost the softball game."

"Which was my fault," Sarah added.

Carolyn smiled gently. She knew about Sarah's lack of athletic talent. "I'm sure no one blames you, Sarah. Erin, there's a letter for you."

"Thanks," Erin said, taking the envelope from her.

Katie, Trina, and Megan went into the bathroom to wash up. Erin sat on her bed and read her letter. Sarah climbed up to her own top bunk and opened the paperback book she'd been reading. She'd just borrowed it from a girl in another cabin. From the cover, it looked like a suspense story. But it had turned out to be very romantic too.

She used to read a lot of romance books, but then she had become tired of them. This one was different, though. Maybe because the characters were just fifteen, only four years older than she was.

She got so engrossed in the story that she jumped when Erin suddenly exclaimed, "Fantastic!"

Sarah looked up. "What's fantastic?"

Erin held up the letter. "This is from my girlfriend back home, Barbara. And listen to this." She read aloud. " 'Sally told me that Jimmy told her that Steve Morris has a crush on you. He wants to know when you're coming back from camp. I'm going to have a party as soon as you get home so you and Steve can get together.' "

"But I thought you already had a boyfriend back home," Sarah said. She pointed to the picture taped on the wall by Erin's bed. "Alan, right?"

"Oh, sure," Erin said. "But it wouldn't hurt to make him a little jealous. Besides, Steve Morris is a major hunk, and the star of the soccer team." She smiled happily. "I can't wait for Karen Jones to hear about this. She's had a crush on Steve for ages. And when it gets back

11

to Alan, he'll be furious!" She sank back on her bed with a very satisfied expression. "They might even have a fight over me."

"That's nice, I guess," Sarah said.

Katie, Trina, and Megan came out of the bathroom. "What's nice?" Katie asked.

"Some boys are going to fight over Erin," Sarah told them.

Trina looked taken aback. "What's so nice about that?"

"You guys wouldn't understand," Erin said. She got up. "I'm going to wash my hair."

"But you just washed it yesterday," Megan noted.

Erin smiled. "Maybe if you washed your hair more often you'd know what it's like to have boys fighting over you." She sauntered into the bathroom.

"That's dumb," Megan said. "Who wants to start fights anyway?"

Katie grinned. "Erin probably thinks it's romantic."

Sarah didn't want to admit it, but she thought it was sort of romantic too. In fact, there was a situation like that in the story she was reading. She went back to her book. But for some reason, she felt restless, and she had a hard time concentrating on the story.

12

I just read about romance, she thought sadly. Erin *lives* the stories. She put the book down and sat up.

Katie was talking. "When the Eagle boys come over here on Wednesday, let's challenge one of their cabins to a swimming relay. I'll bet we could beat them at that."

Trina and Megan agreed with enthusiasm. Sarah didn't say anything. She'd only just learned to swim that summer. She was doing okay, but she wasn't all that good at it. And she doubted she'd be much of an asset in a relay.

Listening to them plan the event was depressing. She climbed down from her bunk and went into the bathroom.

Erin was standing at a sink, rubbing some white cream into her hair.

"What's that stuff?" Sarah asked.

"It's a special conditioner," Erin replied. "You have to rub it in for ten minutes."

"What does it do?"

"It makes your hair very soft and shiny. And it adds body too—makes your hair look fuller."

Sarah fingered her own limp brown hair. It was soft enough. Of course, it would probably look better if it was fuller and shinier. But would she have the patience to spend ten minutes rubbing that stuff into her hair?

13

She perched on the edge of the sink next to Erin's. "Erin, that boy who was sitting at lunch with you and Bobby . . . what's his name?"

"Josh. He's a friend of Bobby's."

"Oh."

Erin looked at her. "Why do you want to know?"

Sarah shrugged. "Just curious."

Understanding lit up Erin's eyes. "You think he's cute, don't you?"

Sarah hoped she wasn't blushing. "Yeah. Sort of."

Erin nodded wisely. "Then go after him!"

"Easy for you to say," Sarah murmured. "You know how to attract boys."

"That's true," Erin said, still rubbing her head. "I guess I'm lucky. It just comes naturally to me."

"I wish . . ." Sarah paused.

"What?"

Sarah felt embarrassed saying this, but she went ahead. "I wish I could attract a boy. I wish I could be more like you."

Erin raised her eyebrows and stared at Sarah in amazement. Now Sarah could really feel her face redden. "I mean, maybe I could learn . . ."

Erin continued to stare, but her expression

14

changed. She seemed to be looking at Sarah as if she'd never really noticed her before.

"I guess that's impossible." Sarah sighed.

Erin cocked her head to one side and eyed her thoughtfully. Then she smiled. "Oh, I wouldn't say that."

Chapter 2

"Who's going on the trip to Pine Ridge today?" Carolyn asked the next day. They were on their way back to the cabin after lunch.

"Not me," Trina said. "I'm taking my campers on a nature walk."

Katie made a face. "That's the problem with you being a counselor-in-training. Now you're going to have to spend the afternoon with a bunch of whiny little kids instead of hanging out with us."

Her remark didn't seem to bother Trina. "They're a pain sometimes, but they're not really whiny. And I enjoy the work." She glanced at her watch. "I better run if I'm going to get there on time. See you guys later."

"Can you believe that?" Katie asked. "She'd rather baby-sit than go with us to Pine Ridge."

"Very weird," Megan agreed.

"I don't think she's being weird," Sarah said. "It's what she wants to do. Just because we're all friends and cabin mates doesn't mean we all have to have the same interests."

Carolyn nodded. "Sarah's right. Like they say, you have to do your own thing."

"Like who says?" Megan asked.

"I don't know." Carolyn laughed. "Someone back in the sixties."

"Well, I'm certainly glad my thing's not baby-sitting," Erin announced.

"What *is* your thing?" Katie asked, grinning mischievously. "Hair?"

"No," Megan answered. "Boys. Can boys be a thing?"

"Well, they're not really people," Katie replied. "So I guess they *are* things." They both started giggling.

Sarah gazed ahead of her, at Erin's hair. It did look awfully nice. She tried to remember the name of that fancy conditioner.

"Are the rest of you girls going to Pine Ridge?" Carolyn asked.

"I am," Erin said.

"Me too," Sarah echoed.

Megan turned to her. "Great! We can go to the skating rink."

17

Sarah bit her lip. "Well, uh . . ." Erin turned her head and gave Sarah a meaningful look.

Luckily, Katie broke in. "Yeah, I'm up for skating."

Sarah breathed a sigh of relief. At least Megan would have someone to go with. She hadn't yet gotten up the nerve to tell Megan what *she* planned to do in Pine Ridge. Mainly, because she could imagine what Megan would say.

Yes, it was better to keep it a secret for now, she decided. Of course, it couldn't be a secret for long.

They stopped at the cabin just long enough to change from shorts to jeans and get their pocketbooks. Then they all went over to the activities hall, where the bus was already waiting. They were a little early, so the bus was empty.

Sarah boarded first. The cabin six girls usually sat up front, but this time she went down the aisle and took a seat in the back. Megan got on next. She looked at Sarah in surprise. Katie was right behind her, and poked her into the front seat. Then she sat down beside her. Erin came to the back of the bus and sat next to Sarah.

Megan kept turning and looking at Sarah, who avoided her eyes. Soon the bus filled up, and Sarah couldn't see her anymore.

"Did you bring money?" Erin asked.

Sarah showed her the contents of her wallet. "I've been saving all summer for some hardcover books I wanted."

"This is more important," Erin assured her. "You read too much anyway."

"How can anyone read too much?" Sarah asked. "I mean, it can't hurt you.'

Erin explained. "It scares boys to see a girl reading. They might think she's too smart for them. Besides, a person who's always reading looks like she's got nothing better to do."

"Oh, right." That didn't really make sense to Sarah. But she figured she'd better listen to her. Erin knew what she was talking about.

During the short ride to Pine Ridge, Erin went over her plans for Sarah. Sarah listened carefully as Erin ticked off each detail on her fingers. It sounded overwhelming to her. And just about as realistic as hitting a home run. But Erin spoke with so much confidence that Sarah could almost believe her plan would work.

The bus pulled into Pine Ridge, and stopped on Main Street. Sarah and Erin got up and joined the line of girls in the aisle. When they emerged from the bus, Megan and Katie were waiting for them.

19

"You want to get some ice cream before we go to the rink?" Megan asked. "Or after?"

"I'm, uh, not going to the rink," Sarah said. "I'm doing something with Erin."

"What?" Katie demanded.

"Just some shopping. We'll meet you guys for ice cream later, okay?"

She couldn't blame Katie and Megan for looking puzzled. Sarah never hung out with Erin in town.

"Well, okay," Megan said finally. "See you at three o'clock at the ice cream parlor."

Sarah and Erin headed in the opposite direction from them. "Where are we going first?" Sarah asked.

"The drugstore. It's right here." They went in and Erin picked up a basket at the door. "Take this." Then she led Sarah to the hair care section.

"Wow, I never knew there was so much stuff to put on hair," Sarah said. "Erin, why are you staring at me like that?"

"I'm trying to decide what you need." She took a lock of Sarah's hair and felt it. Then she examined the products on the shelves. She selected one and handed it to Sarah.

Sarah read the label. "I've already got shampoo."

"This is a special one for oily hair."

Sarah put a hand to her hair. It felt dry to her. But it didn't look like Erin's.

"And you'll need a conditioner." Erin took a bottle of that and dropped it in Sarah's basket. "Now, let's go." She went back up the aisle, and then stopped suddenly.

"What's the matter?" Sarah asked.

"I just had a brilliant idea," Erin replied, gazing at the shelf. Sarah followed her eyes.

"Erin, this is hair color."

"I know."

Sarah gasped. "You think I should dye my hair?"

Erin took a box from the shelf. "Wouldn't you look more interesting with hair this color?"

Sarah looked at the picture of the woman on the box. "It's awfully *red.*"

"That's the idea. Boys really notice redheads."

Sarah tried to picture herself with red hair. Her imagination wasn't that powerful. "But my father would throw a fit! I can't go home with red hair!"

"You won't," Erin said. She pointed to the description on the box. "See? It's not permanent. The color washes out after ten shampoos."

Sarah hesitated. "You really think it would look good?"

"Good?" Erin shrugged. 'Well, of course it's not as sexy as blonde hair. But there's no way to go blonde that's not permanent. And it's definitely better than mousey brown."

Sarah dropped the box into her basket.

"Okay, pay for this and then we'll hit the cosmetics store."

"They've got makeup here," Sarah pointed out.

"There's more variety down the street."

Sarah had to believe her. Erin knew every store in Pine Ridge, except maybe the hardware one. Sarah paid for the hair products, and then they went halfway down the street to the cosmetics store.

"May I help you?" a salesgirl asked.

"She needs a complete set of makeup," Erin said.

The girl looked at Sarah in doubt. "Isn't she a little young?"

"It's actually for her sister," Erin said smoothly. "They have the exact same coloring."

Sarah marveled at how easily Erin could lie. And the salesgirl seemed to buy her story. She scrutinized Sarah's face. "What about a blue eye shadow?"

"I think mauve would be better," Erin said. As they debated the issue, Sarah's eyes roamed the counter. So many colors of everything! How could she possibly choose?

But she didn't have to. Between Erin and the salesgirl, all decisions were made for her. And before long there was a whole row of items laid out—liquid makeup, powder, blush, shadows, eyeliner, and mascara.

The salesgirl added everything up and announced the total. Sarah couldn't believe how much it all cost. "I could have bought an entire library for that," she moaned.

Erin ignored that remark. "How much money do you have left?"

Sarah counted. "Not quite ten dollars."

"I guess we can forget about new clothes." Then she snapped her fingers. "No, wait a minute!" She led Sarah across the street.

"What's this place?"

"It's a second-hand clothes shop. There's a lot of junk, but sometimes you can find great bargains. Don't tell anyone, but I once bought a blouse here for two dollars. Brand-new, it would have cost thirty." They went inside.

There were rows and rows of racks with clothes hanging from them, plus tables with clothes piled on top. Sarah followed Erin around in a daze as Erin went from rack to rack, pushing clothes aside. Skirts, blouses, dresses flew by as Erin rejected item after item.

"That's pretty," Sarah noted, pointing to a flowered dress with a lace collar.

Erin sneered. "It's too babyish. Hey, check this out." She snatched a hanger from the rack. It held a short, black skirt.

Sarah's face fell. "It's kind of plain, isn't it?"

"It's mature. Now, let's find a top." She headed to another rack. "Aha!" She held up a black short-sleeved shirt.

"All black?" Sarah asked in dismay.

"Black is very sophisticated," Erin informed her. "It'll make you look older, and you need that." She thrust the skirt and top at Sarah. "Go try these on."

Sarah took the clothes into the tiny dressing room. She put on the shirt first. It was much harder getting into the skirt. It was very tight.

Erin came into the dressing room. "I don't think it fits," Sarah said, still struggling with the zipper.

"Hold your breath," Erin said. She tugged at the zipper. It finally went up, but Sarah could barely breathe. Her reflection in the mirror didn't make her feel much better.

"I don't think this is my style. It's just not, you know, *me.*"

"Well, that's the whole point, isn't it? You want to change your image, right?"

"Yeah, I guess so. But it's so tight. I don't think I could sit down in it."

"Then don't sit down when you're wearing it," Erin suggested.

"Where am I going to wear this anyway?" Sarah asked.

"There's bound to be an evening get-together with Eagle soon," Erin replied. "And if you just lose five pounds it'll be perfect."

Sarah changed back into her jeans and took the clothes to the cashier. The skirt was five dollars and the top was four. Now she was flat broke. She didn't even have enough money left for an ice cream. . . . Quickly, she looked at her watch.

"Erin, it's four o'clock! We were supposed to meet Katie and Megan at the ice cream parlor at three!"

"You don't need to be eating any ice cream," Erin said reprovingly. They headed down the street toward the ice cream parlor. Erin paused in front of a beauty parlor and looked at a sign in the window.

"Hey, you could get your ears pierced."

25

Sarah's hands flew to her ears. "I don't have any money left."

"I could lend you some," Erin began, but she was interrupted when Megan and Katie ran up to them.

"Hey! Where have you guys been?" Katie asked.

"I'm sorry," Sarah said. "I guess we lost track of the time."

"Well, it's too late for you guys to have ice cream," Megan reported. "It's time to get the bus."

Sarah was relieved, even though she wouldn't be getting any ice cream. At least her earlobes wouldn't be punctured today. The girls headed toward the corner where the Sunnyside bus was already waiting.

"What's in all the bags?" Megan asked.

"Just some stuff," Sarah replied vaguely. "I'll show you later."

The bus was already filled with campers, and the girls couldn't get seats together. Sarah didn't mind. She felt like being alone for a while to examine her purchases.

Sitting in a seat next to some girl who was talking to the girl behind her, Sarah peered inside the bags. Everything had such a pretty name . . . Golden Essence. Misty Rose. Tawny

Beige. Sarah shivered in delight. In these little bags lay all she needed to change her life. She closed her eyes and spent the whole bus ride trying to conjure up an image of the new Sarah.

"We're meeting Trina at the lakefront to take out canoes," Katie announced when they got off the bus.

"I'm going back to the cabin," Erin told them. She looked pointedly at Sarah.

"Yeah, me too."

"Why?" Katie asked.

"We've got something to do," Erin said, and started walking away.

Megan pulled Sarah aside. "What's going on?"

"Don't ask me now," Sarah pleaded. "You'll find out, I promise." She ran to catch up with Erin.

The cabin was empty. "I hope Carolyn doesn't come in while we're doing this," Sarah said.

"She won't," Erin stated. "I heard her say she's got a counselors' meeting and it won't be over till dinnertime. That gives us almost two hours. Take off your clothes and put on a robe."

Sarah did as she was told. While she changed, Erin read the instructions on the hair color box. "This says you're supposed to wash your hair first."

27

Sarah took her new shampoo and went into the bathroom. Before she stuck her head in the sink, she took a look in the mirror. I look so ordinary, she thought. Well, I can say good-bye right now to the boring old Sarah. And very soon, I'll be saying hello to a new me.

She was rinsing the conditioner out of her hair when Erin joined her in the bathroom. "Comb your hair," Erin instructed her, "while I mix this stuff together."

While she pulled the comb through her hair, Sarah watched as Erin opened the box. She pulled out two small bottles and a large, empty plastic one. She poured the contents of the small bottles into the large one and started shaking it.

"Do you think I should change my name?" Sarah asked. "Sarah sounds so—so serious."

"You're right," Erin replied. "You know, my friend Sally's real name is Sarah. Sally's her nickname."

"Really?" Sarah tried it out. "Sally Fine." It sounded like a lively person, like the kind of girl who would be pretty and have dates. "Okay. I'm going to tell everyone to start calling me Sally."

"Are you ready?" Erin asked. "Put a towel over your eyes."

The liquid felt cold and strange on her scalp.

28

She could feel Erin parting her hair, adding more, and combing it through. She did that over and over again, piling Sarah's long hair on her head. "You can take the towel away from your eyes now."

Sarah's hair looked like it was covered with brown slime. Erin took a plastic bonnet from the box and put it over Sarah's head. Then she checked the instructions again. "You have to leave it on for thirty minutes. Let's go for forty-five just to be on the safe side."

They went back into the main room. Sarah walked stiffly, as if her hair would fall out with any sharp moves.

"While we're waiting, I'll give you a manicure," Erin offered. She got a nail file and several bottles from her nightstand drawer. "We need something for you to lay your hands on."

"I've got a big dictionary." Sarah went to the little bookcase and pulled it out.

"I knew books must be good for something," Erin said. She looked over Sarah's hands and frowned. "Your nails are a mess, Sarah."

"Sally," Sarah corrected her. "Erin, I really appreciate this. You're being awfully nice to me."

"I know," Erin said. "This is fun. I feel like I'm remaking you."

Sarah smiled happily. She was perfectly willing to put herself in Erin's hands for remaking.

"Pink or red?" Erin mused, examining her nail polish bottles. Before Sarah could choose, she decided. "Pink. Your nails are too short for red."

Sarah sat very still while Erin labored over her nails. "Erin . . ."

"What?"

"Tell me about what you do on weekends back home."

"Weekends?" Erin's brow puckered. "It's hard to say. I mean it depends on what's going on."

"Just describe one weekend," Sarah insisted. "Like the weekend before you came to camp this year."

"Let me see . . . there was a pajama party Friday night at my friend Julie's." The memory made her smile. "Some boys tried to crash it. They stood outside the window and yelled till we met them on the porch. In our pajamas! On Saturday we went to the mall. Then, Saturday night, there was a preteen dance at the country club. And on Sunday . . . wait, what did I do on Sunday? Oh yeah, Alan took me to the movies."

"Wow," Sarah breathed. "Was that a typical weekend?"

Erin shrugged. "Every weekend's different."

"Not for me," Sarah said. "Mine are all the same."

"You're kidding!"

"Well, not exactly the same. But just about." She sighed. "On Friday nights we go to one of my relatives for dinner. Or they come to our house. Saturday I go to the public library and check out books. Saturday night I baby-sit for a neighbor. If I don't have a baby-sitting job, I go over to my friend Margie's, or she comes to my house."

"What do you and Margie do?"

"Watch TV or get a video or play Scrabble. On Sunday, I do homework. Sometimes my father takes my sister and me out to dinner."

"That sounds pretty boring to me," Erin said bluntly.

Sarah had never thought it was boring before. But now, after hearing all about Erin's weekends, she couldn't help but agree.

Erin looked at the clock on her nightstand. "Okay, it's time!"

Sarah could feel her heart thumping. Unsteadily, she got up and went back into the bathroom.

"It'll be easier if you wash it out in the shower," Erin said. Sarah slipped out of her robe and stepped into a stall. She turned the water on full blast, covered her eyes, and felt the gook falling out of her hair. When she couldn't feel any more of the stuff left, she came out, wrapped her head in a towel, put on her robe and went back into the room.

"How did it come out?" Erin asked.

Sarah gave her an abashed grin. "I didn't look. I was too nervous."

Just then, the cabin door swung open. Katie, Megan and Trina ran in. "You guys missed a great time!" Katie cried out. "We had a canoe race with cabin seven. And we won! Hey, maybe that's what we should challenge the boys to, a canoe race. We were good!"

Trina groaned. "I don't know if I can manage another canoe race real soon. My arms are sore from paddling."

"What have you guys been doing?" Megan asked.

Sarah managed a thin smile. "It's a surprise."

"And you're just in time to see it," Erin told them. "Are you guys ready?"

"Ready for what?" Katie asked.

"Just watch Sarah," Erin said. She went over to Sarah and put a hand on the towel. "One, two, three!" She whipped the towel off her head.

Sarah watched their expressions. They were

32

absolutely identical. Katie, Trina, and Megan were all staring at her with their mouths open.

She turned to Erin. "How—how does it look?"

"Go see for yourself," Erin said.

Sarah got up and went to the mirror. It took her a moment to grasp what she was seeing.

Her hair was wet, and it hung in strings. But it was definitely red. And she looked definitely different.

Chapter 3

Sarah returned from breakfast the next morning with a warm glow. Three girls had come up to her table and complimented her on her hair. They'd said things like, "you look so different," and "you don't look like you." Which was exactly what she wanted to hear.

It made up for her cabin mates, Katie and Megan in particular. Megan had come right out and said she looked silly. Even now, a day later, she was still commenting on it.

"I don't get it. Why did you all of a sudden want to dye your hair?"

"Because I felt like it."

Even their counselor kept looking at her with a disturbed expression. "I don't understand either. It's just not like you to do something like this."

34

"It's not against the camp rules, is it?" Sarah asked.

"No . . . but what is your father going to say?"

"It'll wash out before I get home," Sarah assured her. But in her mind, she was thinking she'd talk her father into letting her dye it permanently. He wouldn't like the idea, but he'd probably go along with it. Ever since her mother had died, when Sarah was just a baby, he pretty much went along with anything Sarah and her sister wanted.

"When are the Eagle boys coming?" Megan asked Carolyn.

"In about half an hour," the counselor said, "so you guys better hurry and straighten up." She went into her little room, and the girls started making their beds.

"I've made up a schedule for us," Katie announced. "We'll have the swimming relay first, then a volleyball game. After that we're having a checkers match at the activities hall."

"Who are we playing?" Trina asked her.

"Justin's cabin." Katie grinned. "I checked them out, and none of them are very tall. We can whoop them at swimming and volleyball."

"Count me out of volleyball," Erin said.

"Why?" Katie demanded. "We need you! You're the tallest in the cabin!"

"You want me in the swimming relay, don't you? I'll need time after that to wash and dry my hair."

"Oh, Erin." Trina sighed. "Just this once, can't you let your hair dry in the sun like the rest of us?"

Erin gave her a look that suggested Trina had lost her mind. "Trina, there are going to be *boys* here today. Oh, and Sarah won't be swimming."

Sarah looked up in surprise. "Why not?"

"There's chlorine in the pool water," Erin explained. "It could turn your hair green. That happened to a friend of mine at home when she colored her hair."

"You mean, she can't go into the pool at all while her hair's red?" Megan asked.

"Unless she wants green hair," Erin replied.

"It's no big deal," Sarah murmured. She tried to hide her dismay. It was funny, in a way. Earlier in the summer, she'd used every excuse possible to keep out of the water. But ever since she'd learned how to swim, she had actually begun to enjoy the morning swims.

36

"But you can play on the volleyball team, can't you?" Megan asked Sarah.

"No," Erin answered for her. "She'll need that time to put on her makeup."

"What makeup?" Katie asked. "Sarah doesn't wear makeup."

"I bought some yesterday," Sarah said. "And Erin's going to give me a total makeover."

"But you'll miss out on everything," Trina protested.

"I can still play checkers." Sarah turned to Erin. "Can't I?"

Erin nodded. "If we finish your makeup on time."

Katie's face was aghast. "This is crazy! Sarah, what happened to your Sunnyside spirit?"

Sarah didn't reply. She'd just remembered something. "Listen, you guys, I've decided to change my name. From now on, call me Sally, okay?"

"Sally?!" Trina, Katie, and Megan exclaimed in unison.

"Yes. I've decided I need a new name to go with my new look."

"That's dumb," Katie said firmly. "Your name isn't Sally. It's Sarah."

Sarah faced her. "Your real name isn't Katie, is it?"

"No. It's Katherine."

"So Katie's just a nickname, right? Well, my nickname's going to be Sally."

"But I've been called Katie ever since I was born! We can't start calling you Sally all of a sudden."

"That's right," Megan added. "I wouldn't feel like I was talking to you."

Trina spoke kindly. "Sarah, it's going to be impossible for us to call you by a new name. Not when we've known you so long. We'd keep forgetting and saying 'Sarah-I-mean-Sally.' And you wouldn't like that."

She had a point. "Okay, I'll stay Sarah. For now." But in the fall, she'd be starting middle school. There would be lots of new kids who wouldn't know her as Sarah.

Carolyn came out of her room and they had their usual inspection. "Look!" Megan called from the window. "They're coming."

Sarah joined her. In the distance, she could see the bus with "Camp Eagle" written on its side. She felt her heartbeat speed up. That boy, Josh, was on the bus. Maybe today, she'd meet him.

"We better hurry up," Katie said. "I told Justin we'd meet them at the pool." The girls started changing into their bathing suits.

"I have to go meet the Eagle bus and show them where to go," Carolyn said. "I'll see you guys later."

Sarah was glad to see her leave. At least she wouldn't have to answer questions about why she wasn't swimming. She was going to have to come up with a lot of good excuses to keep out of the water from now on.

Katie was grumbling. "We're going to have to get a girl from another cabin to make up for Sarah."

"Sorry," Sarah said meekly.

Megan's eyes were wistful. "If you hadn't put that stupid stuff on your hair, you'd be coming with us."

Sarah gave her an apologetic smile. She'd have to have a real heart-to-heart talk with Megan, when they could be alone together. Somehow, she'd make Megan understand what she was doing and why.

She didn't mind being left by herself in the cabin. She went over to the mirror and practiced tossing her hair, like Erin did. But instead of bobbing around her shoulders, Sarah's straight, thin hair just flew into her face. This will take practice, she thought.

She climbed up to her bed and opened her book. As she read, the book took on a whole new meaning. She imagined herself as the heroine, flirting and dancing and surrounded by boys. It seemed like no time at all had passed when the girls returned, towels slung around their shoulders.

"How was the relay?" Sarah asked. She could have guessed the answer from their happy expressions.

"We won!" Katie crowed.

"And you should have seen how they behaved afterwards," Erin said, eyeing her cabin mates scornfully. "Splashing the boys like children. And Katie pushed her friend Justin into the pool."

"You should have seen Erin," Megan said with equal scorn. "Parading around the pool like Miss America in the swimsuit competition."

Sarah climbed down from her bed and joined Megan on hers. "I need to talk to you," she whispered.

"Can't now," Megan said. "We have to change and get over to the volleyball court. Did you change your mind? Are you going to come play?"

"I can't. I have to stay here. Erin's going to help me with my makeup."

Megan rolled her eyes, shook her head, and

40

proceeded into the bathroom. Sarah frowned. Maybe later, when Megan saw her completely made over, she'd understand.

The others left for the game, and Sarah waited for Erin to dry her hair. She watched with interest as Erin held the blow dryer in one hand, and used the other to wrap each lock of hair around a brush. That must be what makes it curl, Sarah thought. It seemed to take forever. Would she ever have the patience to do that?

Erin laid out Sarah's new cosmetics on the bed. "Come sit here by the light. And take off your glasses."

Without her glasses, everything looked blurry. But Sarah didn't have to see. Erin did everything for her. The creams and powders and brushes stroking her face, her eyes, her lips, felt strange.

"Don't fidget," Erin commanded.

"How long is this going to take?"

"Sarah, it takes time to be beautiful. Of course, for some people it takes longer than for others."

"How am I ever going to do this by myself?" Sarah wondered out loud.

"You'll have to practice. Okay, we're done."

Sarah turned to the mirror. All she saw was a blurry image. Quickly, she put on her glasses.

She barely recognized her own reflection. Suddenly, she was older, sophisticated, glamorous. "Oh, Erin! Thank you!"

Erin reached out and snatched off Sarah's glasses.

"Hey!" Sarah objected. "I need those."

"They ruin the whole look. And you're not blind, for crying out loud. I've seen you read without your glasses."

"That's because I'm nearsighted. I can see fine when something's close up. I just can't see from a distance."

"That's okay," Erin said, and grinned. "It's better to be close when you're talking to boys anyway. Now I'm going to fix your hair."

"What's wrong with it?"

"It's too straight. You want your hair to look like mine, right? Then it needs some curl." Erin plugged in her electric rollers. While they heated up, she went through Sarah's clothes. Clutching the black miniskirt, she said, "I don't suppose you've lost five pounds yet."

"Erin! I only bought that yesterday."

Reluctantly, Erin put it back in the drawer. Then she went to the closet. "Wear this."

42

She was holding Sarah's best dress, her navy and white striped one. "But there's a cookout after the checkers match," Sarah said. "I could spill something on it."

"Don't eat," Erin suggested. "You're on a diet, remember? And you'll probably meet Josh today. First impressions are very important."

Sarah spent the next twenty minutes allowing Erin to roll her hair in the hot curlers. She felt like the little tubes were pulling her hair out, not to mention the fact that her scalp was burning. Then she put on her dress.

"You can use my perfume," Erin said. At least, that was one thing Sarah could do for herself. Then Erin took out the curlers, brushed her hair, and applied some sticky gook to it.

"There! You look great!"

Sarah wished she could see for herself, but the mirror was on the other side of the room and she couldn't see from where she was. As soon as Erin's back was turned, she grabbed her glasses and put them on.

It was amazing. Her hair looked almost as good as Erin's. She took off the glasses and stuck them in her pocket.

They left the cabin and headed to the activities hall. Sarah practically tripped over a rock on the path. "Watch where you're going!" Erin exclaimed.

"How can I watch where I'm going when I can't even see?" Sarah asked.

"All right, you can wear your glasses. But take them off when we get there."

The activities hall was full of campers, boys and girls, talking and laughing. All around the room were little tables where checkerboards had already been set up. Sarah's eyes roamed the room for Josh. But she didn't have enough time to spot him before Erin hissed, "Take them off!" Sarah whipped off her glasses and stuck them in her pocket.

The crowd melted into a sea of unidentifiable forms. Sarah didn't even recognize Katie until she was standing right in front of her. "I've got you a partner," Katie said. Sarah followed her to a table.

"Sarah, this is Josh. Josh, this is Sarah."

Sarah felt like her stomach had dropped to her feet, and her knees felt like jelly. "Hi," she squeaked.

"Pleased to meet you," Josh replied.

Sarah practically swooned. He had manners!

"You any good at checkers?" Josh asked.

"Sarah's the best," Katie proclaimed. "She's the smartest girl in our cabin. She beats the rest of us at all the games. The mental ones, I mean."

Sarah stared at the floor. She wished she was farsighted instead of nearsighted. She was all too aware of how cute Josh was.

"Oh yeah?" he said. "So you're a real brain, huh?"

Sarah kept her eyes down. She had no idea how to respond to that. Once again, she let Katie speak for her.

"She's read practically every book that exists. Right, Sarah?"

Sarah mumbled something. She wondered how Josh was reacting to this statement. She didn't dare look him straight in the face to find out.

Someone in the front of the room called, "Players, take your seats. Eagle takes black, Sunnyside takes red." Katie dashed away, while Sarah and Josh sat down opposite each other.

"Begin!" the voice called out.

Sarah focused on the board. Her head was spinning. It dawned on her that she didn't have the slightest idea what to say to this boy, how to act, what to do. Desperately, she tried to remember how she'd seen Erin behave around boys. But her mind was a blank.

All she could do was play the game. What Katie had told Josh about her was right. She *was* good at checkers, and she knew it. She could project moves and work out strategies. So she concentrated on that, and tried to blank out the fact that this incredibly cute guy was sitting opposite her.

The game moved swiftly. Josh turned out to be a pretty good player too, so there was more of a challenge than when she played with her cabin mates. He got crowned first, and he was the first to jump her.

But Sarah struck back. After another couple of moves, she had her own man crowned. And pretty soon, she was able to anticipate Josh's moves, and plan her own accordingly.

"You're good," Josh said with approval. "Do you play chess too?"

"Yes," Sarah said shortly. She didn't want to be distracted from the game. Maybe she couldn't hold her own in softball. But board games were something else. She got so involved, she actually managed to forget she was playing with someone she had a crush on.

And suddenly, there she was, in the perfect position. No matter which way Josh moved, she'd be able to jump his last man. "You got me," he said. He pushed the disk, Sarah jumped him, and the game was over.

Sarah looked up nervously. She knew how Katie always acted when she lost a game. But Josh was smiling. He had a beautiful smile.

"Great game," he said. "I can beat my cabin mates with my eyes closed."

It was on the tip of Sarah's tongue to tell him she could beat hers too. But would he think she was showing off? She couldn't remember ever feeling so awkward, so tongue-tied in her life. Even reminding herself that she had makeup on and red hair didn't help.

"I read a lot too," Josh continued. "I'm into science fiction. What kind of books do you like?"

Sarah opened her mouth, then snapped it shut. She remembered what Erin had said. Boys didn't like girls who read all the time.

But what could she say? She had absolutely no idea what to talk about. And she couldn't just sit here, speechless.

Suddenly, she realized she needed more than red hair and cosmetics before she could handle herself with Josh. Luckily, just then another boy came over and started talking to Josh. As

47

soon as Josh turned away from her, she stood up.

"Excuse me," she murmured. She dug into her pocket and pulled out her glasses. And she hurried away in search of Erin.

Chapter 4

"You *beat* him?" Erin's expression was aghast. She and Sarah were standing outside the activities hall.

Sarah nodded. "I'm good at checkers. You know that. I always beat you guys."

Erin put her hands on her hips. "Well, if you were good enough to win, you're good enough to figure out a way to let *him* win. Honestly, Sarah, weren't you listening to me yesterday? If you want a boy to like you, you can't let him think you're smarter than he is!"

Sarah felt miserable. "I guess I just don't know how to act with boys."

Erin agreed. "You're definitely going to need more help. The boys are leaving after the cookout, and there's free period then. We'll work on your personality back in the cabin."

"But what should I do if he talks to me during the cookout?"

"Just smile a lot, and nod, and agree with everything he says. And take those glasses off!"

The boys and girls were streaming out of the activities hall. Hastily, Sarah removed her glasses and shoved them back in her pocket. The world became a blurry haze again. It was scary. Here she was, in a place that she knew as well as her own home, and she suddenly had no sense of direction.

"How am I going to find my way to the field?" she asked aloud in a panic.

"Just follow everyone." And Erin disappeared into the fuzzy crowd.

Sarah made out a figure approaching her. With relief, she realized it was Megan.

"How was your game?" Megan asked.

"I won." They merged into the group heading toward the field.

"Fantastic!" When Sarah didn't react, she said, "You don't seem very happy about it."

"Well, I was playing against this boy, Josh. He's really cute, Megan. I think I like him."

"So what?"

"So Erin says I should have let him win."

"That's silly," Megan stated. "Hey, why are you so dressed up?"

50

"I just want to look nice. Erin says first impressions are very important." They'd reached the field where the cookout was being held.

Sarah sniffed. There was a smell in the air that she couldn't quite identify. Then it came to her, and her heart sank. "What are we having to eat?"

Megan looked to see what campers were carrying to the picnic benches. "Chili."

"Darn."

"But you like chili!"

"I know. But there's no way I can eat chili. What if I spill it?"

"Why don't you run back to the cabin and change?" Megan suggested.

Sarah shook her head. "No, it's just as well I don't eat it. Erin says I need to lose five pounds." She sat down on a bench.

"You're nuts," Megan said. "And so is Erin. Look, I'll go see if there's anything that doesn't drip for you." She took off toward the table where the food had been laid.

Sarah squinted and tried to see where Josh was. But squinting didn't do much to improve her vision. She got her glasses, put them on, and scanned the crowd, but she couldn't pick him out.

Megan returned with a tray. "There were

51

sandwiches, so I got you three." She handed the plate to Sarah.

"What are you doing with three sandwiches?" Erin stood there, looking stern. "You're on a diet, remember? Don't you want to get into that black skirt? And get those glasses off!"

Sarah put the sandwiches down and took off her glasses. Erin nodded with approval and walked away.

"Why are you letting her push you around like that?" Megan asked.

"She's helping me. You have to admit, Erin knows how to attract boys."

"But that doesn't mean you have to look like her and act like her to get a boyfriend."

"It works for her," Sarah pointed out.

"That doesn't mean it'll work for you."

Sarah shrugged. "It's worth a shot. Hey, is that a boy coming this way?"

"Yeah. Is that Josh?"

"I don't know! I can't see!"

"Then put your glasses on!"

"I can't! What if it's Josh?"

"Well, whoever he is, he's on his way here."

Sarah held her breath. As the figure came closer, he turned into a recognizable person. And Sarah smiled brightly.

52

"Hi, Josh."

"Hi. How come you ran off like that after the game?"

"I, uh, had something to do. Josh, this is Megan."

"Hi," Megan said.

Josh grinned. "Hi. Listen, Sarah, you want to have a chess match next time you guys come over to Eagle? I've got a set in my cabin."

"Chess match?" Sarah repeated.

"Yeah, you said you could play, right? And there's hardly anyone else who plays at my camp."

"Well, I'm not all that good," Sarah mumbled.

"I'm not great either," Josh said. "We'd be a perfect match."

A perfect match. That sounded wonderful. But he was only talking about playing chess, she reminded herself. She wished she could think of something cute and funny to say. But nothing came to her.

"Yeah, well, maybe," was all she could manage.

"I heard we're having another competition," Josh continued. "Some sort of question and answer thing. You know anything about it?"

Sarah shook her head.

"Well, that girl at the checkers match said you were the brains of the cabin. It sounds like something you might be interested in."

Brains of the cabin. That didn't sound very romantic, Sarah thought.

Josh stood there for a minute, as if he expected her to say something. When she didn't, he looked puzzled. "Well, see you around."

"He seems really nice," Megan said. "And he's definitely cute."

"Yeah. I know."

"I thought you liked him," Megan said after he left.

"I do."

"Then why didn't you say anything? You could have asked him to sit with us."

"I couldn't." Sarah groaned. "Megan, I don't know how to act around boys."

"Just act like yourself!"

Sarah shook her head. Megan just didn't understand.

Everyone had taken off for free period. Sarah sat on Erin's bed and listened intently as Erin talked.

"The first thing you have to remember is not to be too friendly. You have to play hard to get."

"But if I'm not friendly, he'll think I don't like him," Sarah protested.

"I don't mean you have to be *unfriendly*. Just be, you know, cool."

"This is very confusing," Sarah murmured.

"I'll show you. Pretend you're a guy, and you want to meet me." Erin went to the other side of the cabin.

Sarah felt silly, but she got up and walked over to her. "Hi. I'm, uh, Joe. What's your name?"

Erin glanced at her briefly. "Erin." She turned away. But then she glanced back, gave her a fleeting smile, and tossed her head. "See what I mean? Show him you're interested. But not too interested. Now you try it. I'll be the boy." She put on a macho swagger as she walked around the room. "Hi, I'm Joe. What's your name?"

Sarah turned away. "Sarah." Then she looked back, attempted a half smile, and tossed her head.

Apparently, it wasn't a perfect imitation. "You look like you have a stomachache. Now, when he tells you about himself, act like you're absolutely fascinated and impressed, even if you're not. And ask him questions."

"About what?"

55

"Like, what kind of sports he plays."

"What if he doesn't play any sports?"

Erin wrinkled her nose. "Then he's not the kind of boy you want to go out with. Now ask me what sports I play."

"What kind of sports do you play?"

"I'm on the football team at school," Erin replied.

"Now what do I say?"

"Something like this." Erin's eyes widened. "Wow, I love football."

"But I don't like football," Sarah objected.

"Fake it! But don't act like you know too much about it." She went into a performance. "I love going to football games." She giggled. "Of course, I don't understand it at all. Maybe you could explain it to me sometime." She giggled again. "But I probably won't understand a word you say."

"That makes me sound like I'm stupid," Sarah said.

"But that's the idea! You have to let him think he's smarter than you are, even if he isn't. Now, I think the Eagle boys are coming over for a movie tomorrow night. And you'll have a chance to see Josh."

"Should I go up to him?"

"No, wait for him to come to you. First of all,

you're going to have to make up for the fact that you beat Josh at checkers. Let me think." After a minute, she lowered her voice and said, "Boy, you really whooped me at the checkers match."

Sarah tried one of Erin's flirty smiles. "I'm really sorry."

"No, no. That sounds like you meant to do it. You have to pretend it was an accident. Say something like, 'I was just lucky. I didn't even know what I was doing! I'm sure if we played again, you'd win easily.' "

"How am I going to remember all this?" Sarah wailed. "It's complicated!"

"No it's not! All you have to do is act dumb and feminine and giggle a lot. Is that so hard?"

"It is for me."

Erin threw up her hands. "Then give up. Go wash your hair ten times, and take off your makeup, and put on your glasses." With that, she marched out of the cabin.

Sarah stood there, thinking. She could go back to being plain, ordinary Sarah. The brain. The girl who spent her Saturday nights baby-sitting and reading, while other girls went to parties.

Or she could be like beautiful, glamorous Erin. What a choice. She ran out of the cabin and hurried to catch up with Erin. "Erin, wait!"

Erin turned. "What do you want now?"

Sarah gave her an abashed smile. "Can we go back and practice some more?"

Just as the girls were finishing dinner that evening, Ms. Winkle went to the front of the dining hall. "I have a special announcement to make. I've been talking to the director of Camp Eagle about our camp competitions. And we've decided that athletic games aren't enough. We need some intellectual competitions too. So we've decided to have a camp bowl!"

The blank faces that greeted this announcement must have told Ms. Winkle no one knew what she was talking about. "You've heard of college bowls, haven't you?" she asked. The campers' expressions didn't change, so she explained.

"Each camp will have a team made up of three people. They'll be asked a question, and the first person to respond will have an opportunity to answer it. If that person misses, the question goes to the other team. Each person who answers a question correctly gets points. At the end of the competition, the team with the most points wins."

"That must be what Josh was talking about today," Megan said.

58

Katie made a face. "Sounds too hard to me. I'd rather have a canoe race."

"How are the team members going to be chosen?" a camper asked Ms. Winkle.

"We're going to hold a test here in the dining hall tomorrow morning," Ms. Winkle said. "Any girl who wants to can take it. And the three girls with the highest scores will make up our team."

Carolyn gazed at her campers. "Is there going to be a cabin six girl on that team?"

"There has to be," Katie said firmly. Then she grinned. "But not me. Tests give me the creeps."

"Me too," Megan said fervently. "I always panic. What about you, Trina?"

Trina shook her head. "I might do okay on the test, but I'd freeze if I had to answer questions out loud in front of people. Besides, we all know who should represent cabin six on that team."

Everyone was looking at Sarah. She couldn't help feeling flattered. "You guys think I should try for the team?"

"Absolutely," Katie said. "You're the smartest one in the cabin. And I'll bet you make all As at school, right?"

Sarah figured there was no reason to fake

false modesty. "Well, yeah. I have a good memory, so I do pretty good on tests."

"It sounds like the perfect competition for you, Sarah," Carolyn said.

Sarah grinned. "Better than softball or volleyball."

"See?" Megan said. "I told you you'd have a chance to show off your talents. And I'll bet you win the camp bowl for Sunnyside."

Everyone was beaming at her. That is, almost everyone. Erin stood up abruptly. "I'm going back to the cabin. Sarah, didn't you say you had to get back too?"

Sarah stared at her. Erin gave her a meaningful look.

"Oh. Right." She got up. "See you guys back there."

As soon as they were out of earshot, Erin said, "Are you crazy?"

"What are you talking about?"

"You can't be on that team!"

"Why not?"

Erin shook her head wearily. "Sarah, think about it. First of all, Josh might be on the Eagle team. Bobby says he's really smart. And even if he's not on the team, he'll be in the audience. Do you want him to see how smart you are?"

Sarah bit her lip. "But . . . but this is my chance to do something I'm good at."

"What's more important?" Erin asked. "Winning a dumb contest or getting a boy to like you?"

Sarah didn't have an answer for that.

Erin faced her squarely. "Sarah, do you want a boyfriend or don't you?"

"I *do,*" Sarah said. "But now everyone's counting on me. If I don't take that test tomorrow, they'll be furious."

"I know, I know. Go ahead and take the test."

"Really?"

"Sure." Erin smiled. "But just don't do too well."

Chapter 5

At breakfast the next morning, Ms. Winkle was making her usual announcements. "We're having a movie by the lake tonight. And we've invited the Eagle boys to join us for it."

Sarah drew her breath in sharply. She looked at Erin, who gave her a thumbs-up sign.

Ms. Winkle continued. "And the test for the camp bowl will be given during the first activity period, here in the dining hall."

Well, at least she wouldn't have to come up with another excuse to get out of swimming, Sarah thought. With her fork, she mashed up her scrambled eggs. For some reason, she wasn't the least bit hungry.

"Sarah, you've barely touched your breakfast," Carolyn commented.

"I just don't have any appetite," Sarah said.

Carolyn looked concerned. "You're not getting sick, are you?"

Sarah shook her head. Out of the corner of her eye, she could see Erin nodding with approval. If she could keep this up, she'd get into that black miniskirt any day now.

"I know why you're not eating," Megan said. "You're nervous about the test, aren't you?"

"A little," Sarah admitted. But it wasn't for the reason Megan thought. She was worried about how she was going to manage to do badly on it.

"I thought you never worried about tests," Katie said.

"Usually, I don't. But this is . . . different."

After breakfast, they went back to the cabin, straightened up, and had inspection. While the others got into their bathing suits, Sarah brushed her hair.

The effect of Erin's hot curlers had worn off, and her hair was in its usual straight condition. She'd have to suffer through the procedure again later, now that she knew the Camp Eagle boys would be coming to Sunnyside's movie by the lake that night.

63

The tension she was feeling must have been showing on her face. "Don't worry about that test," Katie said. "You'll do great."

Sarah couldn't face her. "Maybe. It might be really hard, you know."

"Oh, c'mon, I'll bet you breeze right through it," Megan assured her.

Sarah felt a desperate need to change the subject. "Does anyone know what the movie is tonight?"

"No," Katie said. "I hope it's something scary."

Sarah glanced at Megan. Now *she* looked nervous. Megan hated scary movies. She joined Sarah at the mirror. "If it's scary, will you sit with me?" she whispered.

Sarah nodded. But privately, she hoped the movie wasn't scary. Mainly because she hoped she'd be sitting with someone else.

"I think this camp bowl idea is great for you," Trina told Sarah. "I know how bad you feel about some of the other activities. But this is your big chance."

Erin, coming out of the bathroom, caught the last few words. "It certainly is," she said. "And she's going to make it happen!"

Sarah looked at her in surprise. "What do you mean?"

64

"Tonight! You're gonna do great!"

"The test isn't tonight," Katie said. "It's this morning."

"What test?" Erin asked.

"The test for the camp bowl, dummy!" Megan exclaimed.

"Oh, *that.*" Erin brushed that aside. "I was talking about Josh, at the movie tonight."

"Who's Josh?" Trina asked.

"This boy I kind of like," Sarah admitted.

"And I've been teaching her all my tricks to get him to like her," Erin announced proudly.

"Well, don't be thinking about him while you're taking the test," Katie warned.

Erin smiled at Sarah, and Sarah knew what that smile meant. She *should* think about Josh while she took the test. It would keep her from doing too well on it.

Suddenly, she felt depressed. Why couldn't she have both? Why couldn't she get on the camp bowl team *and* get Josh to like her?

Because that's not the way life is, she thought glumly. You can't have everything. Sometimes you just have to make choices. She just wished she knew for sure that she was about to make the right one.

Carolyn came out of her room. "Sarah, you want to walk over to the dining hall with me?"

"Okay," Sarah said. "What are you going for?"

"I'm a monitor." She gave her an exaggerated stern look. "I'm supposed to make sure you guys don't cheat."

Not very likely in my case, Sarah thought. As she left the cabin with Carolyn, there was a chorus of "good lucks." She was pretty certain Erin wasn't part of it.

"You look worried," Carolyn said as they walked along. "Are you?"

"No, not really."

"Something's bothering you." When Sarah didn't respond, she asked, "Have the girls been teasing you about your new look? Don't let them bother you."

"I thought you didn't like my hair either," Sarah said.

"Well, I was surprised by it. But then I started thinking." She smiled. "I remember when I was your age, I put purple streaks in my hair."

"You did?"

"Mmm. My parents went wild. But I know what it's like to want to do something different. So if the others are giving you a hard time—"

66

"They're not," Sarah interrupted. "I mean, they said stuff at first. But I think they're getting used to it."

"I guess you're just feeling under pressure," Carolyn said. "I can't blame you. It's rough when everyone's counting on you. But just do your best. And if you don't make the team, I'm sure they'll understand."

They'd better, Sarah thought. Because she wasn't going to make the team.

It was an unfamiliar scene in the dining hall. Twelve girls were there, each sitting alone at a table. Sarah sat down at an empty table and waited while a counselor passed out the tests and pencils.

Maybe it will really be difficult, she thought hopefully. Maybe there will be lots of math and science questions. Those were her worst subjects. Then she wouldn't have to try to do badly. It would just come naturally.

But when the counselor handed her the sheet and she read the questions, her heart sank. They were easy. Who was the second president of the United States? Who wrote *Romeo and Juliet?* Even the one math-type question wasn't hard. What are the three types of triangles?

There were twenty questions like these, every

67

one of which Sarah could answer without even having to concentrate. All around her, girls were chewing their pencils and thinking, or writing down answers.

How many would she have to miss to make sure she didn't get picked for the team? She couldn't bear to answer them *all* wrong. She had too much pride for that. Besides, if Carolyn saw her completed test, she'd know something was up.

I'll miss three, she decided. That should be enough. She scanned the questions to find three that she could put the wrong answers to, without getting anyone suspicious.

The second president of the United States, she decided. People were always confusing presidents. She knew the answer was John Adams. But she wrote "Thomas Jefferson."

Number four read "What is the capital of Illinois?" Lots of people thought it was Chicago, but Sarah had memorized all the capitals in the third grade. The answer was Springfield. With a shaky hand, she scribbled "Chicago."

Now, she had to find one more. They were all so obvious, it was hard to choose. Finally, she picked "What is the longest river in the United States?" The Mississippi, of course. But she wrote, "the Nile." If anyone asked, she could always say she'd misread it, and thought it asked for the longest river in the world.

It only took her a few minutes to answer the rest of the questions correctly. She scrawled her name on top, and took it to Carolyh.

"How'd you do?" Carolyn asked.

"Okay, I guess." Unable to meet her eyes, she turned and hurried out.

"How come you're so quiet tonight?" Megan asked her at dinner that evening.

"I guess I'm just tired. That test was pretty hard," she lied.

Carolyn looked at her in surprise. "You thought it was difficult?"

Sarah shifted uncomfortably in her seat. "Well, there were some tricky questions."

"Aw, I'll bet you aced it," Katie said.

Sarah gave her a sickly smile.

"I know why you're quiet," Erin said. "You're thinking about Josh. As soon as dinner's over, we'll go back to the cabin and roll your hair and get you all fixed up."

"You're not going to wear all that gooky makeup, are you?" Megan asked. "It'll be dark at the movie. No one will be able to see your face."

"She should wear it anyway," Erin stated. "It will give her confidence."

For some reason, Sarah felt annoyed. Erin was acting like she was totally in charge of Sarah's life. Then she scolded herself for her thoughts. Erin was only trying to help her. She should be grateful.

"Girls, could I have your attention?"

All eyes turned to the front of the room where Ms. Winkle was standing.

"I would like to announce the names of the girls who will be on the Sunnyside team for the camp bowl with Eagle."

Under the table, Sarah felt Megan clutch her hand. It made her stomach churn. And her thoughts raced wildly. What if other girls did a lot worse than she had? What if she got on the team after all?

But Ms. Winkle's next words calmed her down. "I must say, all the girls who took the test did very well. But we can only have three on the team. And we had one perfect test, one with only one error, and one with two."

Thank goodness, Sarah thought. Ms. Winkle went on to announce the names. "Gina Lewis, from cabin eight. Betsy Silver, cabin nine. And Monica Greene, cabin eleven. Girls, stand up and take a bow."

The dining hall burst into applause. But the clapping from the cabin six table was pretty halfhearted. They all avoided looking at Sarah at first. She put a lot of effort into making herself look depressed at the outcome.

But the worst part was the way her cabin mates behaved. She'd expected them to be angry with her or at least disappointed. But they weren't.

"Well, it's not the end of the world," Katie said.

"We know you did your best," Trina added.

And Megan put an arm around her. "Don't feel too bad."

That only made Sarah feel worse. Gazing around at her sympathetic cabin mates made her wish a hole would appear in the ground and swallow her. To feel better, she looked at Erin, who responded with a quick smile and a wink.

Back at the cabin, Erin plugged in her curlers. "These will take a minute to heat up," she said. "Sarah, do you want some help with your makeup? Let's go in the bathroom. The light's better in there."

Sarah knew the light in the bathroom wasn't any brighter than in the cabin. Erin just wanted to get her away from the others. Sure enough,

71

as soon as Erin closed the bathroom door, she asked, "What are you going to tell Josh if he asks you about the test?"

"I don't know. I guess I could just tell him I didn't take it."

Erin shook her head. "No, someone like Megan might mention it in front of him and then you'd look like a liar."

Sarah thought. "How's this?" She lowered her eyelids, cocked her head, and tried to imitate Erin's sidelong smile. "I took the test, but only because everyone was bugging me to. It was so hard! And no matter what anyone tells you, I'm no genius." She giggled. "I probably had the worst score in the whole group."

"Not bad," Erin said.

"You gotta be kidding."

Sarah opened her eyes and saw Megan standing in the doorway. "What's the matter?"

"What's the matter with *you?*" Megan shot back.

"If it's any of your business, Sarah's learning how to flirt with boys," Erin told her.

"That's not flirting," Megan said, "that's acting like an idiot."

"Don't be so immature," Erin said. "Look, Sarah, I've got to figure out what I'm going to wear tonight. Then I'll come back and help you with your makeup." She left the room, and Megan came closer.

"Why are you pretending you're stupid?" Megan asked.

"Erin says boys don't like girls who are too smart."

Megan's eyes narrowed. "I guess you must be glad you didn't make the camp bowl team. Then Josh would know you're smart."

Sarah swallowed. "Well, yeah. I mean, I'm sorry I didn't make it, but I think it's for the best. If I want Josh to like me, I mean."

Megan stared at her. "Sarah, did you screw up that test on purpose?"

It was on the tip of Sarah's tongue to deny that. But it was so hard to lie—especially to Megan. So she turned away, and looked at her reflection in the mirror above the sink.

Megan took her silence for an answer. "You *did!* You missed questions on purpose!"

A combination of guilt and anger burned inside her. "Well, what if I did?"

"Sarah! I can't believe this! You let us down for—for a boy!"

Sarah turned to her. "Maybe when you grow up you'll understand."

That was the kind of thing Erin was always saying to the rest of them. And it never seemed to really bother anyone. But Megan's eyes were blazing. "You—you traitor!"

"Oh, Megan, give me a break."

But Megan had no intention of doing that. "Don't you feel any loyalty to your camp? To *us?*"

Sarah tried to put on mascara but her hand was shaking. "I didn't do anything so awful."

"I think what you did was awful. And I'll bet Katie and Trina would think so too. Not to mention Carolyn."

She was right. Sarah turned to her with pleading eyes. "Listen, Megan . . ."

"What?"

"Don't tell the others, okay?"

Megan's lips were pressed together tightly.

"We're still best friends," Sarah went on. "And best friends keep each other's secrets."

Finally, Megan spoke. "All right. I won't tell. But I hope you feel really rotten about this." She stalked to the door. "And as far as being best friends, I'm not so sure about that anymore."

Sarah gazed at her reflection. She'll get over this, she told herself. We've had fights before. And when she sees how happy I am about Josh, she'll forgive me.

As for feeling rotten, well, in all honesty, she

couldn't say she felt good. But tonight she'd see Josh. And if everything worked out the way Erin said it would, that would make up for these bad feelings.

She wished Erin would come back right that minute and reassure her, tell her she'd done the right thing. Because the memory of Megan's face lingered. And Megan's words kept ringing in her ears.

Sarah loved movies by the lake. She never even cared what movie was being shown. There was something special about being outside at night, the moon shining on the lake, the summer breeze blowing through your hair. Usually, the cabin six girls huddled together on one big blanket, sharing a huge bag of buttery popcorn.

Tonight was different, though. The Eagle boys were there. Erin had already disappeared in search of Bobby. "Is it okay if I invite Justin to sit with us?" Katie asked.

"Maybe I'll ask Stewart, too," Megan said. Stewart was a boy she played tennis with frequently.

"Sarah, why don't you invite that boy you like," Trina suggested. "What's his name—Josh?"

"Maybe I will," Sarah said. But she didn't think it was a great idea. If Josh hung around with them, she'd feel really uncomfortable doing her Erin act. "I'll go look for him."

She left the group and headed toward the refreshments table, where lots of boys were gathered. Wandering through the crowd, she spotted Josh and eased toward him.

"Hi."

He turned and smiled. "Hi! Hey, this is really neat, having movies outside. We never have anything like this at Eagle."

Sarah nodded. "Sometimes the movies are kind of silly. Like really dumb comedies or cartoons. But watching them outside makes it nice."

"Yeah, as long as it's not something like *Texas Chainsaw Massacre.* I really hate those movies."

"Me too," Sarah agreed. "I can't understand why anyone wants to see a lot of people getting chopped up. I like historical movies, especially ones about real people."

"So do I!" Josh said.

It suddenly dawned on Sarah that Erin would never be having a conversation like this. And she realized, to her horror, that she still had her glasses on. She whipped them off, cocked her head, and gave him a sidelong smile. "Of course, sometimes it's not so terrible watching scary movies. If you're with someone special."

In the dark and without her glasses, she couldn't read his expression. "I guess. Uh, did you take the test for the camp bowl?"

Sarah giggled. "I did, but only because everyone was bugging me to. Of course, I did absolutely awful on it. It was so hard!"

"Really? Ours wasn't. I thought they were giving both camps the same test."

"Well, I'm such an idiot, it probably just seemed hard to me. I could barely answer any of the questions! I probably made the worst score in the whole group."

"You're kidding!"

Sarah giggled again. "I'm just a dummy, I guess."

"I thought you liked to read. That girl—what was her name?"

"Katie."

"Yeah, Katie. She said you read all the time."

"Oh, she was just kidding. I hardly read at all. Just a comic book once in a while." She tossed her head the way Erin did. "To tell the truth, I usually have much better things to do than read books."

"Like what?"

"Oh, you know, parties, dancing, shopping. Just generally having fun."

He didn't say anything. She moved a little closer. Now she could see that he wasn't smiling. He wasn't even looking at her. At the back of the crowd settled on the ground, she saw a counselor putting a reel on a projector.

"I think the movie's about to start," she said. "See that rock over there? It's a good place to sit."

"Yeah, well, I've gotta sit with some friends. See ya." And he disappeared into the darkness.

Sarah stared after him, long after she couldn't see him anymore. Why hadn't he wanted to sit with her? What had she done wrong?

A wave of depression, like a big black cloud, settled on her head. Right this minute, Erin was probably sitting with Bobby, whispering and giggling and maybe even holding hands. And here she was, looking as much like Erin as humanly possible, acting just like Erin—and she was alone.

She couldn't face going back to the blanket where the cabin six girls and their Eagle friends were sitting. Dazed and confused, she made her way to the rock she'd pointed out to Josh, and sat there by herself.

78

She couldn't see the screen at all—it was a total blur. She pulled out her glasses and put them on.

After all, there was no point in looking pretty now.

Chapter 6

The movie was boring. At least, Sarah thought it was. It was supposed to be a comedy, about a family on a trip where everything went wrong. The kids in the family were fighting, the suitcases fell out of the trunk, the father drove around in circles and got lost. It was just one silly adventure after another. And none of it made sense. Even when the car fell off a cliff, the whole family got out without even a mark on them.

This is so ridiculous, Sarah thought. The other campers on the lakefront didn't share her opinion, however. All around her, kids were laughing hysterically, yelling at the characters on the screen, calling out "you jerk" and "watch out!"

Sarah wondered if Josh was one of the kids yelling. Somehow, she doubted that. He just didn't seem to be the type to act goofy. He probably didn't like this movie any more than she did.

But all the cheerful shouting and laughter made her feel even more alone. She climbed off her rock and went in search of Erin. Making her way through all the groups sitting on blankets, she tried to keep from tripping on them and ignored their cries of "out of the way!"

Finally, she spotted Erin with Bobby. They were sitting alone together on a blanket. They probably don't want to be disturbed, Sarah thought. Too bad. This was an emergency.

At least they didn't appear to be engrossed in the movie. They were too busy looking into each other's eyes. For a moment, Sarah stood there silently in the darkness, watching them. It should be her and Josh, sitting like that, their heads together, whispering. What did boyfriends and girlfriends whisper about, anyway?

All she knew was that she wasn't with Josh, and Erin had practically promised her she could make that happen. Well, it wasn't happening. Sarah must have done something wrong, and she didn't have the slightest idea what it was.

"Erin," she hissed. And then she said it louder. "Erin!"

81

Erin turned. The annoyance was clear in her expression and her voice. "What do you want?"

"I have to talk to you!"

The urgency in her voice must have penetrated Erin's head. With a mild show of reluctance, she got up and came to Sarah. "What's the matter?"

"It's Josh," Sarah said plaintively. "Oh, Erin, I don't know what's the matter with him. I did everything you told me to do, and I said all the right things, just like we practiced. But he didn't even want to sit with me!"

Erin frowned. "Were you wearing your glasses when you saw him?"

"No."

"Did you smile a lot?"

Sarah nodded vigorously.

"Hmm." Erin thought for a moment. "Maybe you overdid it."

"What do you mean?"

"You might have come on too strong. Sometimes, if a boy knows you're flirting, he gets scared. You always have to be subtle with them."

Sarah moaned. She had so much to learn! At this rate, she wouldn't have a boyfriend until she was eighty years old.

"There's another possibility," Erin said. "He might just be shy. Hey, Bobby."

The boy on the blanket was into the movie now. Erin had to call him twice before she got his attention. "Huh?"

"Is Josh shy?"

Bobby shrugged. "Nah. He's one of those serious brainy types. Real smart. He's gonna be on that camp bowl team for Eagle."

"Really? He didn't tell me that." Sarah's heart swelled. So he was modest, too. Cute and nice and smart and not a show-off. Not one of those macho, know-it-all guys who gave her the creeps. He was the kind of boy she'd dreamed about, the kind of boy who was perfect for her. There was only one small problem. He wasn't interested in her.

"This camp bowl thing's really dumb," Bobby went on.

Erin nodded. "You are so right. It's too much like school."

"There's going to be a social at Eagle afterwards," Bobby added.

"Neat!" Erin exclaimed. Then she cocked her head and gave Bobby her little half smile. "Hope you find a date."

Bobby grinned. "Yeah, well, I got someone in mind."

Erin arched her eyebrows and giggled. "Anyone I know?"

Sarah could barely keep a straight face. Their conversation was so cutesy it was sickening. But she had to watch and listen. This was flirting. This was what she needed to learn.

Then Erin pulled Sarah aside. "Don't worry. You'll have another chance with Josh at the social." She looked Sarah over critically. "You know, I think you've already lost some weight."

She was probably right, Sarah thought. She'd been feeling so weird lately, she hadn't been eating much.

"I'll bet you'll be able to get into that black miniskirt for the social. And you'll knock his socks off."

"You really think so?"

"Yes," Erin said firmly. "Just don't give up. We'll practice some more, I promise." She returned to her blanket.

That's supposed to cheer me up, Sarah thought. But she didn't feel any more cheerful than she was before. And watching Erin and Bobby huddled on their blanket made her feel even more down. Would all the flirting practice in the world ever bring her and Josh together like that?

She wandered back to her own private rock,

sat down on the ground and leaned against it. She felt something bumpy under her rear, and pulled it out. It was a book. In the dark, it was hard to make out the title, but by holding it up toward the beam from the movie projector she could read the cover. *The Three Musketeers.*

She'd read it last year. It was a good book, and she wouldn't mind reading it again. Usually, she brought a book and a flashlight to the movies by the lake, just in case the movie was dumb, like this one. But she'd been afraid to, in case Josh saw her reading.

Someone else obviously had the same habit she had. Briefly, she wondered who it was. Whoever it was would probably come back for the book. She opened it, but it was impossible to read without a flashlight. And she couldn't go back to the cabin for one. It was against the rules to walk through the camp at night by yourself. So she just sat there, with her knees up, her elbows on her knees, and her chin resting in her hands.

"Why are you sitting here all by yourself?"

Sarah looked up at Megan. "I just feel like it."

"Where's your boyfriend?"

"I don't have a boyfriend."

"Gee, and after all the work you've put into getting one. Too bad."

Megan was never good at being sarcastic. It just wasn't her nature. But Sarah couldn't blame her for trying. In a low voice, she said, "I'm sorry for what I said before."

Megan sat down next to her. After a few minutes of silence, Sarah added, "And you were right about the test."

"What do you mean?"

"I do feel rotten about it. Like I let everyone down. And not just our cabin. The whole camp. But it's good I didn't get on the team. I just found out Josh is on his."

"I just don't understand why that matters," Megan said.

Sarah didn't feel like going into the whole explanation again. "I'm sure the girls who made the team will do okay."

"Yeah, I guess. Listen, what I said about not being best friends anymore . . . I didn't really mean it. I was just angry."

"It's okay," Sarah said. "You had a right to be angry."

"Well, everyone makes mistakes," Megan said. "I guess the important thing is to correct them."

Mistakes . . . Sarah wasn't sure if Megan was

talking about herself or about Sarah. It didn't matter. She might not have a boyfriend, but at least she still had a best friend.

"Did you see Josh tonight?" Megan asked.

"Yeah. I thought he might sit with me, but he didn't want to." She sighed. "It doesn't make sense. I'm doing everything Erin does, but it's just not working. I don't get it. If it works for Erin, why isn't it working for me?"

"Because you're not Erin," Megan replied.

Sarah gazed at her in frustration. "I don't want to *be* Erin. I just want to be *like* her."

Megan didn't answer. She was looking past Sarah. Sarah turned her head.

"Excuse me," Josh said. "I think I left a book around here. Did you see it?"

"Is this it?" Sarah asked, holding up *The Three Musketeers*.

"Thanks." He took it from her.

"Why'd you bring a book to the movies?" Megan asked.

Josh gave her a crooked grin. "I was afraid the movie might be boring."

"That's what Sarah does too," Megan said.

"You do?" he asked in surprise.

Sarah cringed in embarrassment. "Well, like you said, sometimes the movies aren't too good."

"Like tonight," he said.

87

"Yeah, this is pretty silly."

"And this book's good," Josh said.

"I know. I read it last year."

"You did?" This time he sounded even more surprised. "Well, thanks for holding on to it for me. See ya." And he took off.

Sarah buried her face in her hands.

"What's wrong?" Megan asked.

"I did everything wrong!" She ticked off her errors. "I had my glasses on. I told him I'd already read a book he was reading. And I didn't even flirt!"

"He didn't seem to mind," Megan pointed out.

"That's just because he's polite." She gazed off in the direction he'd gone. She'd just gone and blown another chance with him.

Oh well, like Megan said, mistakes could be corrected. And there was still the Eagle social to come.

Carolyn stood in front of Sarah's bunk. Her arms were crossed. "Not swimming again today?" she asked as the other girls tore out of the cabin in their swimsuits.

"I think I'm coming down with a cold," Sarah said. For good effect, she coughed twice and threw in a sniffle.

Carolyn didn't buy her act. "That was a crummy performance, Sarah."

Sarah pulled herself up. "I *can't* go in the water, Carolyn."

"Why not?"

"My hair! Erin says the chlorine in the water will turn my hair green."

Carolyn shook her head wearily. "Haven't you ever heard of a bathing cap?"

"A bathing cap?" Sarah repeated stupidly.

Carolyn went into her room, and emerged a second later dangling a bathing cap by its strap. "Here." She tossed it on Sarah's bed.

Sarah grinned. Clutching the cap, she climbed down from her bunk and pulled her swimsuit from the drawer.

By the time she got to the pool, the action was in full swing. It was a free swim day. Katie, Trina, and Megan were tossing a beach ball around in the water. Erin, as usual, was stretched out on the landing, smoothing suntan lotion on her legs.

"You're not going in the water, are you?" she asked Sarah.

Sarah waved the bathing cap at her. "Carolyn gave me this to cover my hair."

"But it's free swim day," Erin argued. "You

don't *have* to go in. Why don't you lie here and work on getting a tan? You're awfully pale."

Sarah couldn't imagine anything more boring than just lying there and letting the sun beat down on you. "I'd rather go in the water," she said, pulling on the cap.

"Suit yourself," Erin said. "But a good tan always makes a girl look prettier."

Sarah hesitated. Erin's golden skin did look nicer than hers. But the water looked so inviting. And now Megan was yelling, "Sarah, come on in! We can make teams!"

Sarah couldn't resist. She jumped in the water. She and Megan paired off against Katie and Trina, and tried to keep the other team from getting the ball. The game involved a lot of splashing and dunking and shrieking. And for a while, Sarah was able to forget all about Josh, the camp bowl, the flirting lessons. Without any makeup, and with her red hair hidden under the cap, she was just regular Sarah again, having fun with her friends.

When swimming period was over, the girls headed back to the cabin. "It looks like it's going to rain," Trina commented.

"If it does, let's have a marathon Monopoly game," Katie suggested. "We haven't played one of those in ages."

"Sounds good to me," Sarah said.

Behind her, Erin whispered in her ear. "You should use that time to practice putting on makeup. You're going to have to learn to do it yourself eventually."

Sarah tried to conceal her disappointment. She'd much rather play Monopoly than spend the afternoon blending eyeshadows and trying to find her cheekbones so she could apply her blush properly. She was beginning to wonder if a boyfriend was worth all this effort.

But then she thought about Josh, and how much she wanted him to like her. And if that meant slaving over her face, she supposed it was worth the sacrifice.

But when she reached the cabin, all thoughts of makeup and Monopoly and even Josh flew out of her head. Carolyn had a message for her.

"Ms. Winkle wants to see you. Right away."

"Me?" Sarah gasped. Ms. Winkle only summoned a girl to her office when there was a problem. She couldn't think of any rules she had broken. She turned to her cabin mates. But they all looked bewildered too.

"I guess I better go," Sarah said, turning back toward the door.

"I don't think Ms. Winkle will mind if you change first," Carolyn noted dryly.

She'd forgotten she was still in her bathing suit. Quickly, she changed into her shorts and tee shirt and pulled on her tennis shoes. Then she hurried out of the cabin and ran to the camp director's office.

Ms. Winkle was talking to the secretary when she went in. "Yes, dear?" Ms. Winkle called all the girls "dear." Mainly because she could never remember their names.

"I'm Sarah, from cabin six. My counselor said you wanted to see me."

"Oh, yes. Come into my office."

Sarah followed her in, and sat down in the chair Ms. Winkle indicated. "It's about the camp bowl competition with Camp Eagle," Ms. Winkle said.

Sarah gulped. How could she possibly know Sarah had missed questions on purpose? Megan wouldn't have told her. She waited for Ms. Winkle to continue.

"One of the girls on the team has come down with chicken pox. She's in the infirmary, and the doctor says she won't be well enough to participate."

"That's too bad," Sarah said.

"Indeed it is," Ms. Winkle said. "She was the highest scorer on the test. But I went back over the tests, and discovered that you had the fourth highest score."

Sarah stared at her dumbly. She knew what was coming.

"So this means you'll be on the team, representing Sunnyside." Ms. Winkle announced this with a big smile, as if she expected Sarah to let out a cheer.

But Sarah just froze. "Me? On the camp bowl team?"

"That's right, dear." She looked puzzled, probably because Sarah's reaction wasn't what she expected. "I know you must be feeling a little nervous, since you didn't do as well on the test. But that doesn't mean you're not as smart as the others on the team."

Sarah managed a sickly smile. Ms. Winkle didn't know she could have made a perfect score if she'd wanted to.

"Are you sure I've got the next highest score?"

Ms. Winkle nodded. "You only missed three questions. The next highest scorer after you missed five." Her forehead wrinkled. "Don't you want to be on the team, dear?"

"Oh, uh . . . sure. I guess."

Her hesitancy didn't bother Ms. Winkle.

"Fine. I know you'll do your very best, and you'll make us proud of you."

"I'll—I'll try," Sarah stammered.

She left the office in a state of shock. She was going to be on the Sunnyside camp bowl team. Josh was going to be on the Eagle team. They'd be competing against each other. And if Erin was right, that was the worst possible position she could be in.

It's not the end of the world, she told herself. Okay, he's going to know you're smart, because you're on the team. But at least you can make sure he doesn't think you're smarter than him. Just because you're playing opposite him doesn't mean you have to win.

Chapter 7

Sarah was so lost in thought when she left Ms. Winkle's cabin that she didn't even realize it had started to rain. When the light sprinkle turned into a downpour, she raced back to the cabin.

Inside, the girls were setting up the Monopoly game. "Sarah, you're soaked!" Carolyn exclaimed. "I'll get towels and you get out of those wet clothes." She hurried into the bathroom.

Her cabin mates were interested in something more important than Sarah's damp condition. They fired questions at her.

"What did Ms. Winkle want?" "Are you in trouble?" "What did you do?"

"I didn't do anything and I'm not in trouble," Sarah replied as she pulled off her wet clothes and wrapped herself in a robe. Carolyn emerged from the bathroom with a towel and began rubbing Sarah's head. Erin came over and peered at her closely.

"Your hair's beginning to get a little mousier. We'll have to get more of that color."

Hair was the last thing on Sarah's mind. "Erin, I can't think about that *now.*"

"Tell us!" Megan demanded. "What happened?"

"One of the girls on our camp bowl team has chicken pox. I had the next highest score. So I'm going to be on the team."

Shrieks and cheers filled the room. Megan threw her arms around her. "That's fantastic!"

Katie was dancing around the room. "Absolutely, positively fabulous!'

"We're so proud of you!" Trina chimed in.

And Carolyn was beaming. She ran into her private room and came out with a box. "I just got this today and I was saving it for the weekend. But we deserve a celebration now!" She placed it on the floor and opened it. "Cupcakes, cookies, brownies, and assorted treats with no nutritional value."

Katie was still hopping up and down. "We're going to mutilate Eagle!" she crowed.

Only Erin wasn't joining in the general cheer.

"Sarah, your hair is still wet. Come in the bathroom and use my blow dryer on it."

Sarah avoided her eyes. "That's okay. I'll just dry it with the towel."

"It'll dry faster with my blow dryer." Erin's voice was insistent.

"Erin's right," Carolyn said. "You shouldn't sit around with a wet head when you've just had a chill."

"Yeah, we want you good and healthy for the camp bowl," Katie noted.

"Don't worry," Carolyn added, "we won't eat everything before you're back!"

That wasn't exactly what Sarah was worried about. "C'mon," Erin said, grabbing her hand. She practically dragged Sarah into the bathroom.

"Are you crazy?" she asked as soon as the door closed. "You can't be in this camp bowl! Didn't you hear Bobby say that Josh is on the Eagle team?"

"I know," Sarah moaned. "But what could I do? Tell Ms. Winkle I refuse to be on the team?"

Erin switched on her dryer and handed it to Sarah. "How good are you at pretending to be sick?"

Sarah remembered her feeble attempt at faking an illness with Carolyn that very day. "Not

97

good at all. Look, Erin, there's no way I can get out of this. I'm just going to have to be on that team, and that's it."

Erin shook her head sadly. "You really disappoint me, Sarah. And here I thought you were serious about changing your life."

"I *am* serious!"

"You're not even drying your hair properly! I showed you how to do it. You have to bend over and dry from underneath the hair to give it body."

Sarah wasn't in the mood for beauty instruction. She switched off the dryer and handed it back to Erin. "It's dry enough now."

Erin paced the bathroom floor. "I can't believe this. After all I've done for you, just to help you get a boyfriend. I colored your hair, I showed you how to put on makeup, I've taught you how to flirt—and now you're blowing it all away because of some stupid camp contest! All that hard work for nothing."

A wistful note crept into Sarah's voice. "Erin, do you really think being on this team is going to ruin my chances with Josh?"

"It's certainly not going to help."

In her mind, Sarah watched all her fantasies slip away, like sand castles on a beach after the tide comes in. The sadness she felt must have been evident on her face, because Erin's tone softened.

"Okay, maybe it's not the end of the world. You managed not to do too well on the test. You could do the same thing in the camp bowl."

"Screw up?" Sarah asked faintly.

"Don't answer too many questions. No guy likes a show-off. And you could always throw in a few wrong answers. Whatever you do, don't make Josh look bad. Like, if he answers a question wrong, don't volunteer the right one. It'll seem like you're putting him down and he'll feel stupid. Especially in front of all those other guys."

"I'd never want to do that to him," Sarah cried out in horror.

"Then be careful. He's going to know you're smart because you're on the team. Don't make things any worse than they already are."

Megan burst into the bathroom. "Hey, what's keeping you guys? We're having a party out here!"

Everyone was gathered on the floor, going through the goodies in Carolyn's box. Sarah was reaching for a cupcake when she felt Erin's hand on her arm. "Black miniskirt," she mouthed. It took a lot of willpower, but Sarah withdrew her hand.

99

"Do you have any idea what the questions are going to be like?" Trina asked.

"No," Sarah said. "If the contest is like the test, they could be about anything."

"What we need is an encyclopedia," Katie remarked. "Then we could quiz you."

"Now don't put pressure on Sarah," Carolyn warned her. "You can't really study or practice for something like this. Sarah will just have to rely on what she already knows."

"Besides," Erin interjected, "Sarah's got something else to practice."

"What?" Katie asked.

"There's going to be a social at Eagle after the camp bowl. And there's a certain boy there."

"Really?" Carolyn looked at Sarah with interest. "Well, that explains the hair and the makeup. Who is he?"

"His name's Josh," Sarah said.

"And he's on the Eagle camp bowl team," Megan added.

"What a great coincidence!" Carolyn said. "You'll have a good opportunity to impress him!"

Impress him? Sarah gazed at Carolyn in wonderment. For an older girl, a woman really, she certainly didn't know much about boys.

* * *

100

"What's the capital of North Dakota?" Katie called to Sarah.

Sarah winced as Erin pulled the hot rollers out of her hair. "Pierre."

"That's *South* Dakota!"

"Oh, yeah. Bismarck, right?"

"I thought you had all the states and capitals memorized!" Katie yelled. "You're not going to get any second chances, you know."

"I was just teasing you," Sarah hastily replied. She hadn't been, though. She had just been making sure she *could* give a wrong answer.

Erin started brushing Sarah's hair. "North Dakota, South Dakota . . . what's the big deal? Sarah, your hair's going to look great. Be careful, Megan. You're making a mess."

Megan made a face, but she didn't say anything. Erin had talked her into helping by touching up Sarah's chipped nail polish. Sarah knew that Megan thought all this beauty stuff was dumb but had agreed to help because she was still feeling bad about their fight.

Trina laughed. "It will be awful if she misses a question, but it'll be a real disaster if her nail polish is smeared."

"But she's not going to miss questions," Megan said. "Are you, Sarah?"

Her voice was unusually serious. Sarah

101

couldn't look her in the face. "I'll try. I mean, I'll try not to."

"Okay, what's the population of the United States?" Katie asked.

"Now you guys stop that," Carolyn chided. "You're going to make Sarah nervous."

"They won't make me nervous," Sarah said. "I've already done that to myself."

"I'll do your makeup," Erin said.

"Thanks," Sarah said, looking at her gratefully. There was no way she could do it for herself. She'd have eyeshadow on her cheeks.

Erin had just finished spraying her with perfume when it was time to leave. Sarah put on her glasses.

Erin looked appalled. "You're not going to wear those, are you?"

"Why shouldn't she?" Katie asked.

"Because Josh is going to be there," Erin replied. "And she looks better without them."

"But I think better with them on," Sarah murmured.

"You don't have to think that well," Erin whispered in her ear. She was right, Sarah thought. She took the glasses off. And they all left together.

The dining hall had been transformed. Tables had been removed, and chairs were set up in rows. It seemed like the entire population of Eagle and Sunnyside was there, milling around, talking, and claiming seats. Up on the stage there were two long tables, with three seats behind each.

"What are those things on the tables?" Megan asked.

"I don't know," Sarah replied. "They look like light bulbs."

"Will everyone please take a seat?" Ms. Winkle called out from the stage. "And contestants, please take your places up here at the tables."

Megan clutched Sarah's hand. "Good luck," she whispered. "I know you'll do your best." Sarah responded with a weak imitation of a smile.

Up on the stage, she greeted the other two Sunnyside contestants, Melissa and Gina. She couldn't resist sneaking a peek at the Eagle table. She could tell that Josh's face was turned in her direction, though without her glasses she couldn't see his expression. But she suspected he must be pretty surprised, especially since she'd told him she'd done badly on the test.

She took her seat and looked out into the audience. Now she was glad she wasn't wearing her glasses. At least this way, all those people out there were just a fuzzy blur. And she wouldn't be able to pick out her cabin mates. She wouldn't have to see their reaction to her performance.

Ms. Winkle spoke from the center of the stage. She welcomed the audience, and went on to introduce the contestants, the judges, and the counselor who would be asking the questions. Then she explained the rules.

"The contestants each have a switch in front of them. The switch turns on their light bulb. The first contestant with a lighted bulb will have the opportunity to answer the question. If that person fails to answer the question correctly, there will be ten seconds for a contestant on the other team to respond. With each correct answer, a team gets five points. With each incorrect answer, five points are subtracted."

She paused to let all this sink in. And then she added, "So don't take wild guesses if you're not sure, because it could cost you. Now, contestants, are you ready?"

There was a general bobbing of heads.

"Then begin!"

The counselor read off the first question. "Who invented the telephone?"

That's easy, Sarah thought. And sure enough, the words had barely left the counselor's mouth before a light went on at the Eagle table.

"Alexander Graham Bell."

"Correct. How many ounces are in a pound?"

Sarah squirmed. She knew that one too. And she was going to have to answer some questions or she'd really look like an idiot. But the girl next to her had already hit her switch. "Sixteen!"

"Correct. Whose picture is on a penny?"

Gina's light lit up. "George Washington."

"Wrong. Eagle?"

Sarah heard Josh's voice. "Abraham Lincoln."

"Correct. What is the planet farthest from the sun?"

"Pluto."

"What is the largest planet?"

"Mars."

"Wrong. Sunnyside?"

"Jupiter," Melissa said.

"Correct. Who invented the cotton gin?"

Sarah's hand developed a mind of its own. She hit the switch. "Eli Whitney."

"Correct. Who wrote *Little Women?*"

Sarah's hand moved again. "Louisa May Alcott."

"Correct. Who were the characters in *The Wizard of Oz* who accompanied Dorothy on the yellow brick road?"

An Eagle boy got his light on first. "The Scarecrow, the Tin Man, and the Cowardly Lion."

"Wrong. Sunnyside?"

That wasn't wrong, Sarah thought. And then she realized what the boy had missed. Her bulb lit up. "The Scarecrow, the Tin Man, the Cowardly Lion, and Toto the dog!"

"Correct!"

The questions seemed to come faster and faster. And Sarah gave up all efforts to pretend she didn't know the answers. She was smart. She knew that, and her friends knew that. And Josh was bound to find that out sooner or later.

"Who gave a famous speech which began 'I have a dream'?"

"Reverend Doctor Martin Luther King, Junior," Sarah responded.

"What makes plants green?"

Sarah reached for her switch but she wasn't fast enough. An Eagle contestant gave the right answer, chlorophyll. Darn, she thought. The one science question she could have answered.

"What famous event occurred on April 18, 1775?"

She got that one. "Paul Revere's ride."

"Who was the first woman to cross the Atlantic Ocean in an airplane?"

What luck! Sarah had written a paper about her just last year in school. "Amelia Earhart."

Now she wished she had her glasses. She'd have liked to see her cabin mates' faces, glowing with pride. On the other hand, she wouldn't really like to see Erin's expression.

The questions kept coming. Sarah knew a lot of the answers, but sometimes someone else beat her to the switch. She could hear Josh answering a lot of the questions too.

"What do we call a book that's the true history of a person's life?"

Gina had the answer. "Biography."

"What is the highest mountain in the world?"

An Eagle boy took that one. "Mount Everest."

It was exciting. The score was close. "What is a book of maps called?"

Sarah hit the switch. "An atlas."

"Where were the first Olympic games held?"

"Greece." That came from Sunnyside.

"How many players are on a soccer team?"

She heard Josh reply, "Eleven."

More questions. More bulbs lighting up. More answers. And then the counselor stopped. "The score is now sixty-five to sixty, in favor of Eagle. And this is the last question."

The entire room fell silent. If Eagle got this

one, they'd win. If Sunnyside got it, there would be a tie. Well, at least that was better than losing. Sarah's hand hovered over the switch.

"What is the real name of the author of *Tom Sawyer?*"

Sarah's hand fell on the switch, but she was too late. A light on the Eagle side had gone on first. And then she heard Josh's voice. "Mark Twain."

"Wrong. Sunnyside?"

Sarah's hand remained on the switch. She could answer this. And Sunnyside would win. But if she hit that switch, she'd be doing exactly what Erin had warned her about—showing Josh she knew something he didn't. She'd embarrass him in front of all these people. He wouldn't want anything to do with her, ever again.

Of course, she didn't have to answer the question. She could pretend she didn't know. No one would blame her. Only she would know that she'd let down her friends, her camp, all the people who really mattered.

All these possibilities raced through her mind in a matter of seconds. But even as the choices presented themselves, she knew deep in her heart there was only one real choice.

She hit the switch. The light went on. And then she spoke. "Samuel Clemens."

"Correct! Sunnyside wins, sixty-five to sixty!"

A roar went up from the crowd. At the Sunnyside table, the contestants leaped up and practically crushed Sarah in a hug. Within seconds, they were joined by Katie, Megan, and Trina, all screaming and hugging and jumping up and down. Then Carolyn was there too.

She felt her hand being shook, her cheek being kissed, her back being slapped. She was the heroine of Sunnyside. For the first time ever, she'd helped win a major competition.

Sarah loved every minute of it. She felt proud and happy and good about herself. As long as she didn't think about a certain person over at the other table.

Chapter 8

"I think the Eagle team's coming over to congratulate you," Trina said, peering over Sarah's shoulder.

Sarah couldn't bear the thought of seeing Josh. Not after she'd just humiliated him. No matter how polite he was, his dislike was bound to show on his face.

"Let's get out of here," she said. She pushed her way through the crowd toward the exit, and her friends followed her. When she emerged outside, she saw Erin.

It was almost as hard facing her as it would have been to face Josh. Erin didn't say anything, but she didn't need to. She just stood there, shaking her head, her hands on her hips, her lips set in a tight line.

"Wasn't Sarah incredible?" Megan enthused.

"Incredible," Erin repeated, but her tone gave the word an entirely different meaning. She tossed her head and marched off ahead of the others.

"What's she acting so snotty about?" Katie asked.

Sarah explained. "She thinks I destroyed any possibility of romance with Josh."

"Big deal," Katie snorted. "It was worth the sacrifice. Look what you've done for Sunnyside."

"And for myself," Sarah added. "I'm getting a kick out of being a winner for a change!"

"Is it a bigger kick than you got from dying your hair?" Megan asked, grinning.

Sarah considered that. "You know, I think it is."

"Where's Carolyn?" Trina asked as they entered the cabin.

"She had to stay and help put the dining hall back in order," Katie reported. "Where'd Erin go?"

"I'll bet she's in the bathroom getting ready for the social," Trina said.

Erin came out of the bathroom with a towel wrapped around her head. "You guys better start getting ready. The buses leave for Eagle in half an hour." She went to the closet and started going through her clothes.

"Sarah, what are you going to wear?" Megan asked.

"I don't know."

Erin spoke with her back to them. "If I was Sarah, I wouldn't go."

"Why not?" Katie asked.

"I know why," Sarah said. "I don't think the Eagle boys will be very happy to see me. One in particular."

"So what?" Katie made a face. "If there's anything I hate, it's a sore loser."

Sarah couldn't help smiling, thinking about how Katie acted when she lost a game. "It's okay. I really don't want to go."

"But you don't want to stay here by yourself," Trina protested.

"Carolyn will be here. And I've got a book to read." As she said that, she realized she was actually looking forward to being alone and reading. Looking at Erin, with the towel covering her wet hair, gave her another idea. "And there's something else I want to do too."

"What?" Megan asked.

"You'll see." Grabbing her robe from the hook by her bed, she went into the bathroom. She stripped off her clothes and stepped into a shower stall.

The instructions on the hair color box had said the color would last through ten shampoos. She'd washed her hair twice since coloring it. This was going to be a hair-washing marathon. She just hoped she had enough shampoo.

She lathered her hair, rubbed harder than usual, and then rinsed the soap out. Then she did it again. And again. She counted off each shampoo. After eight times, she washed it twice more, just for good measure.

When she finally came out of the stall, her head burned from all that scrubbing. She pulled on her robe, and with her hair dripping, she went directly to the mirror over the sink.

Erin came in. She took one look at Sarah, and gasped. "What did you do?"

"Washed the color out of my hair."

"I can see that. Well, I guess there's no reason for you to try to look pretty anymore."

Sarah considered her reflection. "I don't think I look so bad." She started combing out her tangles.

Erin stood at the next sink and started applying her makeup. "I can't believe I wasted all that time on you."

"Sorry about that," Sarah replied. "I guess I

113

owe you something. You know what? I'm going to give you all the cosmetics I bought."

She left the bathroom. Back in the main room, all the girls were dressed for the social. Carolyn was there too. "How nice you all look," she was saying. "Sarah, you'd better hurry."

"I'm not going."

"Are you not feeling well?"

"I'm fine. I'd just rather not go."

Carolyn frowned. "Well, that presents a problem. Ms. Winkle just asked me to be a chaperone. And you know the rules. You can't stay here by yourself."

Erin emerged from the bathroom. "I'm ready," she announced. "Let's go."

"Sarah needs to dry her hair and get dressed," Carolyn said. "Speaking of which, I'd better change too." She disappeared into her room.

"You're going to the social?" Erin asked in surprise.

"Looks like I don't have any choice," Sarah said.

"You're going to have to face Josh sooner or later anyway," Megan noted.

"I suppose you could always hide in the bathroom there," Erin suggested.

Suddenly, without warning, Sarah felt a surge of anger flow through her. "I'm not hiding in any bathroom. And if Josh is embarrassed, well, too bad for him. I wouldn't want a boyfriend like that anyway. Can I borrow your hair dryer?"

Erin was so stunned by her outburst she just nodded dumbly. Sarah grabbed the dryer and marched into the bathroom.

Sarah stood by the refreshment table, adjusted her glasses, and gazed out at the crowd. She noticed a girl in a black miniskirt, just like the one Erin had made her buy. She could have worn that skirt tonight. But she hadn't wanted to. She had a feeling she'd never wear it. It just wasn't *her*. That skirt was bought for a girl with red hair who acted silly. It wasn't for Sarah.

And then she saw Josh. He was wandering through the crowd, and he seemed to be looking for someone. Any minute now, he'd see her. And then what? Would he give her a dirty look? Would he just pretend she didn't exist? Would he turn and walk off in the opposite direction?

He didn't do any of those things. He was coming right toward her. "Sarah!"

"Hi, Josh."

"Where'd you disappear to after the camp bowl? I wanted to congratulate you."

Sarah gazed at him suspiciously. Was he being sarcastic? No, his expression was completely innocent. And he didn't look humiliated either.

"You know, I was floored when I saw you were one of the contestants," he went on. "Especially after you told me you did a crummy job on the test." He grinned. "I'll bet that was just an act you were pulling to put me off guard."

Sarah managed a smile. "You're right. It was an act."

"You were terrific!" Josh said. "I'll bet you scored more points for your team than any of the others. I was really impressed."

There wasn't the slightest trace of anger in his voice. No dislike or humiliation. Just honest-to-goodness admiration.

"You were?"

Josh nodded vigorously. "Hey, you look different."

"I know."

"I mean, different in a nice way."

Sarah's head was swimming. "Thank you."

"Uh, I'd ask you to dance, but I'm a pretty crummy dancer."

Sarah smiled. "I'm not very good myself."

"I've got a better idea," Josh said. "Let's get some food and go into the game room. There's a chess board set up in there."

"That sounds great!"

"That's what you say now." Josh winked. "But I plan to get even after what you did to me at the camp bowl!"

Together, they collected some sandwiches. As they crossed the room, she saw Erin, surrounded by boys. But this time, she didn't feel one pang of envy.

Okay, maybe she'd never have a life like Erin's. Maybe she'd never be beautiful or glamorous. She'd always be Sarah, with plain straight brown hair and glasses. Sarah the brain.

But maybe that was an okay person to be. Josh seemed to think so. And so did she.

MEET THE GIRLS FROM CABIN SIX IN

CAMP SUNNYSIDE #8
TOO MANY COUNSELORS
75913-6 ($2.95 US/$3.50 Can)

In only a week, the Cabin Six girls go through three counselors and turn their cabin into a disaster zone. Somehow camp without their regular counselor, Carolyn, isn't as much fun as they thought it would be.

*Don't Miss These Other
Camp Sunnyside Adventures:*